CORAL

LOVING A WINSTON SERIES
BOOK FIVE

STACY EATON

CHAPTER ONE

CORAL

The last thing I wanted to be doing was sitting on an airplane flying to the other side of the country—especially with my entire family.

However, that was where I was, and despite feeling miserable, I was forcing myself to smile and laugh because that was what they expected of me.

Most people would be thrilled to be going on vacation, especially since we were traveling on a private plane and heading to an incredible house surrounded by some of the best skiing trails the United States had to offer—but I wasn't.

All I could think about was that by the time I returned home, I probably wouldn't even have anything left there for me. No one knew this, but my business was in trouble.

I had always known I wanted to be a business owner, but it wasn't until after college that I decided I wanted to own a coffee house. I went to school to study business and worked many odd jobs during those years. When I was working for ski patrol in the Poconos, I finally decided which direction to go. The day it opened, I had been flying high and thought all the hard work and calculated decisions would pay off.

I had even sourced the perfect coffee bean that I roasted myself. I loved roasting my coffee, but I should have thought twice about what machine I had bought. I invested almost ten grand in that machine to get professionally roasted beans, but that stupid thing was out of warranty and was constantly breaking down. They wanted another grand to extend the warranty a few years.

When I finally opened my doors, I assumed the worst was over, and now I could kick back and enjoy it. Granted, I knew I would still have to work hard, but getting all the pieces together was downright stressful. Unfortunately, I had been very wrong. The stress only continued, and it got more burdensome by the day. Inventory, employee issues, bills, and customers seemed to overwhelm me daily. It had been so difficult that I thought about giving up at least once a week.

Only our family never gave up, and I would never hear the end of it if I did. I could imagine my father shaking his head at me, his eyes sad as he realized I had not only wasted years but tens of thousands of dollars.

I didn't want to disappoint him, but I knew I would in the end. I glanced away from the window where I had been staring at the clouds and shifted my gaze around the plane's interior.

Not only would I disgrace my family by failing, but I would be doing it alone. All five of my siblings had fallen in love, married, and were moving forward with building their families. I didn't even have the time or energy to think about dating.

I'd had plenty of chances, as I'd been hit on many times at the café, but I'd turned down every single one because I had to focus on my business. I was determined to do everything possible to turn it around and make it profitable. I had to prove to them and myself that I could do it.

Every one of my siblings was thriving—not just in love but in their careers. Ethan was a sergeant and a detective; Evan was the head of his nursing department; Carmen owned a

2

psychology practice; Candy was a structural engineer, and Cara was a helicopter pilot and flight medic. Plus, each of them had impressive spouses and children, too!

Even my father had found someone new to share his life with, but me? I was married to my coffee shop—and it was a relationship that was heading for divorce.

I sighed as I watched Carmen lean toward Tim and kiss him. They kept their heads together briefly and whispered before cracking up. Carmen glanced at me, and I wondered if I had been the butt of their joke.

It wouldn't surprise me. I always felt like I was on the outside looking in at my own family. I had felt that way most of my life, but recently, it had gotten worse.

Candy and Carmen would routinely come to the café for coffee, but I was always working, and they were always chatting away, laughing, and planning their lives. I would watch them sometimes, and pangs of jealousy would eat at my insides. If I approached them, they would try to pull me into the conversation, but I felt it was always half-hearted, and then I would get called away again, and they would resume their fun discussions.

Alaina, Evan's wife, slipped into the seat beside me. "You okay? You're very quiet."

"Yeah, I'm just exhausted." I laughed. "I worked extra hours to ensure everything was taken care of before I left."

She squeezed my hand. "You did, but now you can relax. Why don't you close your eyes and rest? We have about four hours before we land."

"Probably a good idea," I replied, and she slipped out of her seat and headed toward the back of the plane. I glanced around the sleek private plane again. Alaina owned it, and I had been on it one other time when she had flown us to a remote island for their wedding.

That was almost two years ago, the last time I had taken time off from my café. It had been the start of a nightmare I had tried to keep waking up from but couldn't seem to do.

I collected a set of headphones from the back pocket of the seat and plugged them into the plane's sound system. Using the controls on the back of the chair in front of me, I found a selection of music to listen to, and I closed my eyes and settled back.

I didn't want to be on vacation, but if I had to be, I would at least take advantage of the time to sleep—and ski. I couldn't wait to hit the slopes again.

MY FATHER WOKE me several hours later, and I blinked groggily as I tried to escape the stupor I had been in. I honestly hadn't slept quite that well in a long time, and I felt like I had a heavy dark cloud around me as I stretched in my seat. I cleared my throat. "Yeah, what's going on?"

"We are about to land. Look out the window." He pointed toward the small oval window, and I peered through the small opening at the majestic snow-covered mountain peaks in the distance. I smiled, feeling something positive for the first time since we left Pennsylvania.

"It's pretty," I remarked.

"Just think, tomorrow, you can be up there skiing down."

"Yeah, it will be nice to do that again."

"How long has it been?"

I shrugged. "I don't know. Maybe four or five years. I wonder if I'll even be able to do it anymore." It was probably longer than that, but I didn't want to admit it. I knew that I hadn't been skiing since I opened the café. Any time before that seemed decades ago.

He patted my arm. "I'm sure you can. You were always good at it. It won't take you long to be flying down the slopes."

I glanced at my father. "How do you know I was any good? You've never seen me ski."

He grinned. "I didn't have to see you to know you would be good. You've always excelled at everything you do."

I looked away from him quickly. "No, I don't."

He laughed. "Of course you do." He patted my arm. "I have to return to my seat. Silvia isn't a fan of landing."

He disappeared as everyone got situated back in their seats. Tim's son, Tripp, slipped into the seat beside me. Besides Tim's kids, I was the only one traveling single.

Ironically, this whole vacation idea had been a gift from my siblings. They wanted me to get away, relax, unwind, and have some fun. When I didn't seem thrilled by it and made no plans to use their gift, they turned it into a family vacation the week of Thanksgiving and guilted me into coming. How could I not come? Everyone would be here—except Cara and Bryan who had work obligations.

I watched the plane descend to the tarmac, and then we taxied to a private terminal off to the side of the airport in Reno. Originally, Alaina wanted us to fly right into Lake Tahoe, but the weather was too tumultuous for that, so we landed in the desert of nearby Nevada and would take rented SUVs into the Sierra Nevada Mountains that surrounded the lake.

I had been skiing in many places, but I had never been here, and although I wasn't excited to be on vacation with my entire family, I was starting to look forward to being on the slopes again. I looked forward to the crisp air, the wind on my face as I flew down.

I had done some research, too, and learned that the area we were staying in was twenty minutes away from several different ski lifts and a host of trails.

While my siblings contributed to the trip, I knew Alaina and Evan had paid for most of it. There was no way we could have afforded the six thousand a night cost of the house we were renting alone. I would have been happy to stay at a hundred-dollar-a-night hotel, but Alaina wouldn't allow that.

When we landed, I turned airplane mode off on my phone and nervously waited for my notifications. The plane did have Wi-Fi, but no one would tell me the code. They all said I was on vacation and needed to unplug. They had no clue how difficult that was for me or how much I needed to stay in touch with things back at the café.

I had nine emails and three texts. The texts were from Monica, my assistant manager. The first one said: *Things are going well.* The second one stated: *The catering order was picked up with no problems*, and the third one read: *Things are still going well. Stop worrying and enjoy your vacation.*

I chuckled slightly; she knew me well. I quickly typed to her to say we had landed and I would now be available if she needed anything.

A few moments later, she told me to turn my phone back off and enjoy myself.

If only I could. I followed everyone out of the plane and assembled in the airport. It took a little while, but finally, we had our luggage, and Alaina, Evan, and Tim went to collect our rental cars.

"I wish Cara and Bryan were here," Candy said.

"I know," Carmen replied. "But she's due any day."

"You know, if you hadn't had a miscarriage, you wouldn't be here either," Candy said softly.

"Yes, I know," Carmen said sadly, then put her hand over her belly. "But this pregnancy will be better."

"I hope so," Candy replied before hugging Carmen.

I turned away from them. I had barely known that Carmen was pregnant the first time before she lost the baby. Most of my siblings had known much earlier but never thought to tell me. When she lost the baby a week later, I felt sorry for her but didn't feel as overwhelmed as most of my siblings, who were more attached to the idea. Unlike my family, I never thought of kids. It wasn't in my cards, so why even consider it?

However, Carmen did; five months later, she was pregnant again. I learned it early, but only because she switched to decaf coffee at the café. Now, she was only two months along, and while she had come on the trip, she had already said she wasn't skiing. I didn't blame her.

We split into three vehicles since there were fourteen of us. The five couples, and then Tim's three kids who had extensive skiing knowledge, plus me. The younger children had remained home with several of the Young family members to look after them.

We made a little train as we drove through Donner Pass, and the farther we traveled into the mountains, the more I began to relax. The first time we went around a curve and saw the lake surrounded by the beauty of the mountains, we had to pull over and get out.

We all stood along the guardrail and let our gazes wander from one side of the lake to the other. It was magnificent.

It took longer to get to our house than planned because we kept stopping and getting out to check out the scenery, but finally, we pulled down the driveway to a large house that sat directly beside the lake.

Everyone went into the house to check out the accommodation, but my feet led me to the water's edge, where I stared in wonder at the sight before me—not just the water but the mountains and the snow that surrounded the body of water. It was literally the most beautiful thing I had ever seen, and for the first time in a long time, I felt a peace descend over me as tears leaked from my eyes.

CHAPTER TWO

LANDAN

"That last one was an awesome run," my brother said as we piled our gear into the back of the Range Rover. "Did you hear the chatter on your skis when you came down? You were going so fast that I could hear them twenty feet behind you." Lance laughed as he slapped me on the back.

"Yeah, I heard it, but I was more focused on not hitting all the Jerrys who appeared on the hill. I don't know what they think they are doing trying to ski that route. They had no right to be there. Those were expert-level slopes. They are going to kill themselves." I chuckled.

"I know. I almost took one down myself. It would have served them right. They should be up at Heavenly or something."

"It's good that we came out when we did."

"Weather was dicey this morning, but with all the fresh champagne on the slopes, it was worth it," he stated, using the slang term for fresh, crisp snow.

"Yes, it was," I replied as I climbed behind the wheel of my vehicle. "I couldn't resist after the dump we got last night."

"We're gonna get something to eat, aren't we? I am so hungry my stomach is eating itself." I glanced at my brother; he was only a year younger than me.

"We can grab a snack, but you know Mom told us to be home by four for dinner."

"A snack? I could eat a four-course meal and still eat again when we got home."

I laughed. "After today, I think we could use some extra calories."

He glanced at his watch after he pulled off his ski jacket. "We've been skiing for over eight hours."

I grinned at him. "And it was awesome."

He laughed. "I can't remember the last time I spent eight hours on the slope, can you?"

"Unfortunately, yes," I replied. I knew precisely when the last time I had been on the slope from the time it opened until the time it closed, fourteen hours to be exact. It was almost one year ago today. It was the day after I was supposed to have walked down the aisle.

All I wanted to do was get lost in the ride and work out all the anger I had inside of me. I came out at seven a.m. and didn't leave the slopes until nine that night. When I finished, I somehow made it home and collapsed into bed. I slept twelve hours and could barely move the next day. I had hoped my mind would have been clearer, but Eve's image and the shit that went down at our wedding were still there.

I realized then that nothing could rid me of that shitstorm if fourteen hours on the slopes couldn't. I had to learn how to block it out, and eventually, I was able to.

Lance grunted. "Oh, yeah, I can remember the last time you did that. Have you heard from her?"

"Hell no, and I hope to God that I never do."

"You know that they broke up, right?"

I frowned and squeezed the steering wheel as I pulled out of the lot. "I couldn't care less what she does."

"What about Aaron? He was your best friend. Have you spoken to him since then?"

"No, and I don't plan to do so either."

"It's a shame. I still can't believe they did that to you."

"Lance, can we not talk about this? It is the last thing on my mind for once, and I'd like to keep it that way."

"Yeah, sure, sorry."

I nodded, not replying, as he took his cellphone out of his pocket and started messing with it. "Luna is home," he said. He held his phone out in front of me so I could see a picture of her with her arms wrapped around Leo and Lucas.

We had a big family. Including my parents, there were ten of us, and we'd been blessed to have the world at our fingertips. There were no handouts. We earned our allowances, trips, cars, education—all of it—by working hard.

My father, London Lancaster, was a top-of-the-world real estate broker. He only handled the most prominent and flashiest of deals. Not that he was big or flashy. My father would rather drive a pickup and wear shorts and flip-flops than go around in a limo and wear expensive suits.

I learned all my business smarts from him and worked closely with him at Lancaster International.

My mother, Lucy, had married my father when she was nineteen. She had me when she was twenty and was as devoted to my father as she was to every one of the kids—all eight of us.

I was the oldest and about to turn forty later in the week. Lance was only a year behind me and had just turned thirty-nine. Our sister, Luna, was behind him and would turn thirty-eight in January. Then there was Leo. He was thirteen months behind Luna.

In under five years, Mom had given birth to four children. Her delivery with Leo was difficult and we almost lost her, but they saved her life after giving her an emergency hysterectomy. I was only five then, but I remembered her being sad and crying when she thought we weren't watching her.

She still cared for us, but even I knew as a young child that something wasn't quite right with her. That all changed two years later when they brought a baby girl named Lily home. I had been confused since I knew what it looked like when Mom was pregnant, and I had difficulty understanding where this baby came from. At first, I wasn't sure I wanted another baby around, but seeing my mother happy made my father happy, which made us all happy.

Two years later, when I was seven, Mom and Dad came home with another baby girl named Laney. I accepted her a little quicker and thought that was the end. Two boys and four girls, and we had a big family.

That wasn't the case, though, because four years after Laney joined our family, Lucas came home wrapped in a light-blue blanket, screaming his lungs out. To this day, he's still the loudest of the bunch.

There was one final addition to our family, and he came two years later. I was twelve by then, and when Levi entered our crew, I was almost as enthralled with him as my parents were. He was quieter than most of the other kids, and we learned he had a few learning disabilities as he grew, but that was caused by being the baby of a junkie.

So now we have a family of ten. Life growing up was as normal as it could be with eight kids going in different directions, but somehow, my parents managed to make it to almost every sporting event, music recital, and play any of us were in.

Three of us have been previously engaged but never made it to the altar, and two said the 'I do's', but ended up in divorce court.

Our parents might be the perfect couple, but the rest of us were having a hell of a time finding the right person. It was sort of a joke with us now, and when we started dating someone new, we barely introduced them to our family because we knew it probably wouldn't last.

I drove the slick streets of South Lake Tahoe, heading back to my parents' home beside the lake. It was an enormous cabin right along the water with an incredible view. Built to look like a log cabin—and then some—it had four floors, a six-car garage, ten bedrooms, twelve bathrooms, two kitchens, an indoor pool, two hot tubs, and two boat slips on the water. There was also a room off the garage that most people would have called a gigantic mudroom, but to us, it was nicknamed the fun closet. In there, we kept all our winter and summer gear. All of us skied. Some, like Laney and Lucas, also snowboarded, and we paddle-boarded and kayaked in the summer months when the water was warm enough not to cause hypothermia. We also had a few boats between us, although those were not in the fun closet.

Last year, after the wedding rehearsal from hell, I returned to Lake Tahoe and remained here. Before that, I had been living in Santa Monica but was not interested in returning there. Most of my business was handled from a distance, and if I had to travel, I could get to Reno International Airport in about an hour.

I loved living in Lake Tahoe. During the winter, I could get to any number of slopes in under an hour and spend the day flying downhill and clearing my head. In the summer, I was out on the water, relaxing with friends I had met around the area. Sometimes, friends from the outside would visit, but I mostly preferred to keep outsiders out of this world. It took a special kind of person to see Lake Tahoe for what it truly was—not just a beautiful location to visit but a magical place that could heal the soul.

That was why I came here and decided I would never leave. Lake Tahoe would be my home until I died. Yes, I would leave to attend to business, and I would visit other places, but this was where I wanted to be—always.

"Lucas just arrived too," Lance said, breaking me out of my thoughts.

"I thought he wasn't coming until tomorrow," I replied.

Lance shrugged. "He probably got an earlier flight."

My parents went between here and Los Angeles monthly; the rest of the kids lived around the country. Laney was the farthest in New York. All the kids were returning to the lake to celebrate Thanksgiving and my birthday.

My parents joked that my birth was the start of our family, and it should be celebrated. Not that the rest of their birthdays weren't, but mine always seemed slightly bigger. This year, it was a huge deal since I was turning forty. Forty!

When did I get so old? And how did I get so old without having someone to share my life with? You would think that because I was a decent-looking guy with a great job and a good sense of humor, I would be able to find someone, but no. Most women only wanted me for my money or my name—which was ultimately my money.

I learned early in life how to spot the gold diggers and who was my friend and not trying to use me for something. Eve was the one case where I had missed the signs.

We pulled down the long driveway from the main road, and the house came into focus. It never stopped surprising me when I saw it, and I knew it was one of the most glorious houses on the lake. During the summer, people on boats would constantly pause in front of the house and take pictures of it. We didn't even bat an eye now. Instead, we'd wave, sometimes inviting them to throw a line to the dock and join us for a beer.

That was the hospitality of the lake. Those who lived here understood it.

I parked my Expedition in front of one of the garage doors as the front door opened and Luna came running out. She threw her arms around me, hugging me tightly. "Man, I wish I could have gone out with you guys today. I tried to get an earlier flight but couldn't."

"That's okay. We are getting more snow this weekend. We'll take you out to Kirkwood after it falls." I peered past her through the trees and noticed three large SUVs parked in front of the house next door. It looked like Dad had rented out the guesthouse for the week.

The guesthouse was almost as big as our house. Instead of ten bedrooms, it only had seven, and there were only nine bathrooms, not twelve. The rest of the house was impressive and not as imposing as ours. It didn't have an indoor pool like ours, but it had one nice twelve-person hot tub instead of two.

Luna helped Lance and me gather our gear from the back of the vehicle as she told us about her trip. As we walked toward the entrance to the fun closet, something caught my eye, and I paused and turned.

Standing near the water was a woman in a blue and orange ski jacket. Her long brown hair lifted from her head like ribbons caught in a breeze. The rest of her seemed frozen in place. I skimmed my eyes over the lake and inhaled, allowing the healing air to fill me. Perhaps that was what she was doing, too.

I smiled as I turned away, hoping she found what she needed.

CHAPTER THREE

CORAL

"What are you doing out here?" Silvia asked a few minutes later.

I turned to her, breaking out of the trance that I had been in. It hadn't been a bad trance. I'd just let myself be, breathing in and out and focusing on the water and the view. The only sounds were the wind in the trees and the occasional car in the distance.

For the first time in a very long time, I allowed myself not to think about anything and just stood there, letting my eyes drift over the beauty before me. It followed the peaks and valleys of the mountain range as they shifted over the wooded land across from me and created a mirror image on the smooth-as-glass water before me.

The only movement other than my eyes was my lungs expanding on the cleanest air I had ever breathed and the life-sustaining muscle in my chest beating much more relaxedly.

"Sorry, I got mesmerized by the scenery."

Silvia touched my arm, gracing me with a beautiful smile. She was a wonderful woman my father had met not long ago. Her eyes were dark brown, and her hair was golden instead of gray. She had lost her husband and three children, and my father quickly fell for the soft-spoken, gentle woman. I knew my mother would have approved of her because she was as strong as my mother had been and just as loving—not only to my father but to all of us. There wasn't one of us who didn't welcome her into our family with open arms.

"It is mesmerizing," she stated, putting her arm around my back. "I can't believe I have never been here before. Archie would have loved this."

Archie was her husband, who had passed away from colon cancer three years ago. "I'm sure he would have. I can't believe I haven't been here either. This was always on my list of places to come to, but I never made it here."

"Well, you are here now, Coral, and wow, those mountains are high. Are you sure you can ski down those?" Silvia asked a bit worriedly.

I chuckled. "Yeah, I can. I started skiing in middle school and skied every day for about four years. I worked on the ski patrol up in the Poconos after college. I have probably come down close to a thousand times."

"I can't even imagine coming down once." She chuckled. "I'm not sure this old body could even handle the bunny slope."

I pulled her toward me. "I'm sure you could handle that, but there is no reason you must. There are quite a few lodges around the area that have wonderful drinks and fires to keep you warm while others ski."

"I'll just bring a book and find a cozy place to sit, or Carmen and I can shop."

"Carmen will love that. Did Dad decide if he was going to ski?"

"He said he'd try it, but he's pretty rusty. Let's hope he doesn't fall and break something."

"Yeah, that would be bad," I replied.

"Not that I want to drag you from this beauty and your peace, but we are getting ready to cook dinner."

"How are we cooking dinner? We haven't gone to the store."

She raised a brow. "How do you think? Alaina had a personal shopper pick up everything that we would need. The fridge and pantry are filled with everything possible."

"She never forgets a thing, does she?" I frowned.

"What's with the frown?" Silvia asked.

"Nothing, but wouldn't it be nice to have that much money that you never had to think or worry about things?"

"I don't know, Coral. I think having that much money can be a burden of a different kind. People always want something from her. I have heard many stories about how people always have their hand out to her and expect her to help them."

"Yeah, I bet." I sighed and gave one more longing look over the lake. Luckily, we would be here for a week, and I could enjoy the view as much as I wanted. "Well, we better go inside and help in the kitchen."

The two of us strolled arm in arm back to the house, and when I stepped in, I froze as my jaw dropped. "Holy crap! Do people really live like this?"

The house before me was incredible. There was a three-story entrance, with a balcony on the second and third floors, where you could see the lake. A large formal dining room was off to the left, and to the right was a huge living room with furniture I'd be afraid to sit on. The room looked like it had come out of the gallery showroom—one I wouldn't be caught dead shopping in because of the cost. My furniture was more along the lines of secondhand and lovingly picked to be functional, not picturesque.

"It is something, isn't it?" Silvia commented from beside me.

"Yeah, it's something alright," I muttered, shaking my head and following Silvia farther into the house. My head snapped back and forth as we passed elegant hutches and chairs. The floors were smooth, shiny wood coated with a lacquer to protect them from scuffs and scratches.

She turned into an archway, and I paused at the door. Carmen, Candy, Riley, and Alaina were all inside, bustling about, looking in cabinets and pulling things out.

"Holy crap, this kitchen is enormous!" My jaw dropped a bit.

"What I wouldn't give to have a kitchen like this," Riley replied, and Carmen laughed.

"Why? You don't cook, Ethan does."

Riley shrugged. "Maybe if my kitchen were this nice, I'd want to be in it to help him."

"What can I do?" I asked as I stepped forward.

"Nothing," Candy stated. "You need to find a place to relax and do that."

I frowned. "You don't want my help?"

"No, we have everything under control," Alaina said. "Why don't you go explore the house? The guys are down the hallway playing pool, and your bedroom is on the top floor on the left side at the end of the hallway. You have the best view."

I wanted to help, but like usual, I was getting shunned from the room. As I turned away, I noticed Silvia frown slightly. Perhaps she understood that I had wanted to stay there with my sisters.

I guess it wasn't a big deal. This trip was my birthday present, and my siblings were allowing me to take advantage of not doing anything. As I wandered toward the living room, I heard them all begin to laugh, and my heart ached slightly, once again feeling left out.

I heard the men down the hallway, but I turned toward the stairs and climbed. I went straight to the top floor and followed the hallway to the left until I reached the end. When I stepped in, my eyes went wide. The entire wall was glass, and the glorious view of the lake was behind it.

I glanced around briefly as I walked toward the wall. My

suitcases were sitting beside the dresser, and there was a door to the side where I could see a shower. The room was done in green, teal, and blue, all soothing to the soul.

I stood by the glass and immediately realized a balcony was beyond the wall. I found the edge of the slider and let myself out. It was windier here, and I was glad I still had my jacket on. I stood against the rail and stared out over the lake.

My heart sighed as I grasped the wooden railing and soaked up the atmosphere. It was incredible here, absolutely stunning, but it was more than that. It was like just breathing in the air and allowing my eyes to drift around somehow repaired the weariness I felt inside.

An image of my mother popped into my head, her smile so warm and inviting, and I closed my eyes to cherish it for a few seconds before I was disturbed by my beeping phone. It was a text from Carmen saying that if I wanted to help, I could.

I asked if they needed me, but she said she didn't want me to feel left out. Yeah, well, that boat sailed quite a while ago. I told her thanks, but I was relaxing outside on my balcony.

I slipped my phone into my pocket and sat down in one of the dark-brown-painted Adirondack chairs. They didn't need me or want me down there. I wondered who thought I might be feeling left out. I had a feeling it was Silvia. She seemed to pick up on that kind of thing. They sure didn't usually.

I leaned back and closed my eyes, allowing the sounds of the trees around me to lull me into a feeling of seclusion and warmth as I burrowed deeper into my coat and got comfortable. My mother's image returned to me, and I suddenly realized it was a memory. She was sitting in the center of her garden, her face turned up to the sun, her eyes closed, and she wore the most serene smile I had ever seen.

God, I missed her. I skimmed my gaze around the area. I bet she would have loved it here.

I continued to let my mind drift, and it twisted around

thoughts of the café at home, my family downstairs, memories of my mother, the cold breeze touching my face, and the fresh air filling my lungs. It swirled and swirled until, finally, I slipped off to sleep.

I woke abruptly when I heard a motor off to the left side and leaned forward. There was another house over there that I hadn't even noticed. It was even more significant than this one but very similar in design.

Near the garage, there appeared to be three men standing around a few snowmobiles. A deep voice echoed through the trees toward me, but I couldn't make out the words. They were just far enough away that you knew they were talking loudly but couldn't make out what they were saying.

Two of them climbed on, and someone else got on the other. A few minutes later, a woman ran out and got behind him, and they turned the snowmobiles around in the driveway and took off around the house. I listened to the sound of the motor as it faded into the stillness of the evening, smiling as it did.

I had always loved riding on the snowmobiles at the skiing resort. We would take turns checking the trails at the end of the day to ensure no one was left behind or stranded somewhere. It was freeing to fly over the frozen earth and bounce over the drifts and hills.

Why had I stopped skiing? Why had I stopped doing everything that I had once loved?

I frowned. I knew that answer well. One day after skiing, we were sitting around the lodge, having coffee, which tasted horrible. I had decided then that I wanted to open a coffee shop. Initially, I thought I would open one there at the resort, but I didn't have the experience or the money to do it then.

So I moved back home and started working my ass off to save every penny I could to build my dream. The plan was to save up, move back to the ski resort, and open a coffee shop. Only that never happened. When I researched it again later, it was still way out of my price range, and I settled for opening one in my hometown.

That would have been all well and good, but then the strip mall owner kept upping the lease, and Chantel stole thousands of dollars from me while I was on vacation. Plus, one of the big chain stores opened only two blocks away from me, and they had a drive-thru. That wasn't even an option for me.

That memory of Chantel instantly brought back my anxiety, and I pulled out my phone and called Monica. By now, the café would be closed, as they were three hours ahead of us.

She answered on the second ring, chuckling, "I was wondering when I would hear from you."

"Sorry, I got here, and we were busy."

"Coral, you are on vacation. There is no reason for you to apologize. Everything back here is fine. Today's receipts were a little higher than normal." She quoted the numbers and told me how much she had deposited on the way home and a few other numbers that she knew I would want.

I began to relax again. "Okay, that sounds good."

"How is it?"

"It's amazing, absolutely incredible."

I could hear the happiness in her voice as she replied, "I am so glad to hear that. You work harder than anyone I know. You deserve time off. I want you to stop worrying and start enjoying yourself."

"Don't worry, I will."

"And catch up on your sleep," she replied.

I chuckled. "I took a long nap on the plane, and I am sitting on my balcony now and drifted off to sleep again."

"Good, you deserve it. Just don't fall asleep while you are skiing down those mountains."

I glanced around as something hit my hand and realized it was starting to snow again. I grinned. "Don't worry, my adrenaline will be flying high. No chance of sleeping on the slopes."

"Good, enjoy it and send me some pictures!"

"I will," I told her and then said goodbye. Before I could forget, I took a few pictures of my view and then of my suite and sent them to her. She was in awe and told me to keep sending them.

I stared out the window one more time, feeling calmer than I had in years, and then I tossed my jacket to the bed and went to find my family. I was determined not to be left out anymore tonight.

4

CHAPTER FOUR

LANDAN

I stood at the window and watched the woman by the water. I wasn't sure what it was, but something about how she stood there called to me. I couldn't see her face or anything else about her, but it was almost like I understood her as she stared out over the water. Was she mourning something or merely enjoying the scenery?

An older woman joined her and stood with her arm around her. Probably her mother, and it only further cemented my thought that she was being consoled.

"Whatcha looking at?" Lucas asked as he paused beside me.

"Nothing really, just a couple of women out by the water."

He chuckled. "Checking out the women, huh? That's a good sign."

"Not for that, numb nuts. I just noticed them, that's all." I smirked in his direction. "I'm not in the least bit interested in finding another woman."

"Mom has snacks in the kitchen, and a few of us want to head out on the snowmobiles before it gets too dark. You want me to bring yours out?"

"No, I think I battered my body enough today."

He punched my arm. "You're getting old, Landan."

"I might be turning forty, but I can still kick your ass on the slopes, Lucas."

"Ha! Won't be long before I'm kicking yours." He walked away, and I glanced out the window to see the two women heading inside.

I followed him into the kitchen, where the gang stretched around the twenty-foot island. Food was everywhere, and I reached over Luna's head to grab something.

"Hey! Don't drop crumbs in my hair." She swatted me away.

"I'm not," I replied around a mouthful of crab dip.

"If I smell seafood later, I will blame it on you."

I grinned at her and moved down the counter to get something else. "Who is staying at the guesthouse?"

My father perked up from where he was seasoning meat. "A friend and her family."

"Yeah, who?"

"You remember Alaina Buckworth?"

"Yeah, sure. I heard Alaina got married and moved east."

"She did, and she brought her family here to celebrate something. I think there are fourteen staying over there."

"I should go say hello to her," I commented.

My mother touched my arm. "I was going to go over in a little while and make sure they didn't need anything. You can come with me and carry the goodie basket."

With that decided, I retrieved a beer from the oversized fridge and sat down to catch up with my siblings. Thirty minutes later, Lucas, Laney, Leo, and Lance went out to get a couple of snowmobiles ready, and my mom gathered a basket of goodies to take to the guesthouse.

I hadn't seen Alaina in a long time, but our paths had crossed more than a few times in business. She was a shrewd business-woman and quite beautiful, too. I was happy to hear she finally found someone and was in a good relationship. I hadn't liked the guy she was with previously.

I carried the large basket filled with treats, wine, and hot chocolate down the path between the houses. As I walked, I wondered if I would see the woman who had been standing by the water. Not that I cared about getting to know her, but I wanted to know who she was and see if my guess had been correct.

Mom rang the bell, and we could hear voices on the other side. A man pulled back the door, and behind him was a young man I recognized—or thought I did anyway.

"Hi, can I help you?"

My mother stepped forward and spoke cheerfully. "Good evening, we are the house owners. We live next door. We wanted to welcome you and make sure you didn't need anything. Is Alaina here?"

He grinned. "She is. Come in and I'll get her." He stepped back. "I'm Evan, her husband."

"I'm Lucy Lancaster, and this is my son, Landan."

We shook hands, and Evan called out loudly to Alaina as the boy near him said, "You are friends with my dad."

"Who is your dad?"

"Tim Kohl."

"Seriously? Tim's here?" I paused as a name came to me. "Wait, are you Dean?"

He grinned widely and nodded. "Yeah, I'll go get my dad."

"Holy crap!" I said to my mom. "I didn't expect that."

Alaina stepped into the foyer. "Lucy, Landan! It's great to see you guys." She came forward and hugged us both as I handed the basket off to her husband. "This house is fantastic. Thank you so much for allowing us to stay here."

"London was so happy to hear from you. He hoped we might find some time to get together or have dinner one night."

"We would love that. Come in, and I'll introduce you to everyone."

"They brought us a gift basket, too," Evan said, holding it up.

Alaina grinned. "Thank you! We can never have too many snacks in a house with this many people, but you already know that." We all chuckled.

"Is everything to your liking?" my mother asked as we followed Alaina toward the kitchen.

"It's perfect," Alaina said, and Tim walked in from around a corner.

"Holy shit! I couldn't believe it when Dean said I knew the man at the door," Tim called out when he saw me. "I haven't seen you in years, Landan."

Alaina stopped. "You guys know each other?"

"Oh, yeah." Tim laughed. "We used to ski together when Emily and I came out. Emily didn't like to go on the higher slopes, so one day, I ran into Landan, and we tag-teamed our way down. Ended up spending a lot of time together after that."

I laughed as I slapped palms with him and pulled him in to hug. "It's been a while." I paused. "I was so sorry to hear about Emily. I was in New York when you had the funeral. I wish I could have been there."

"Thanks, I appreciate that."

An older man stepped into the entrance. Beside him was the older woman from earlier.

"Lucy, Landan, this is my father-in-law, Richard Winston, and his girlfriend, Silvia."

Oh, so not the woman's mother, I thought. We shook hands, and then I turned to Tim. "So, how did you get here?"

He glanced around as if looking for someone. "Dean, any idea where Carmen is?"

"In the kitchen," he stated. "I'll go get her."

"Are the other kids here?" I asked Tim.

"They are. Why don't we go in the kitchen and you can meet everyone else."

We followed Alaina and the rest of the people toward the kitchen, chatting about the last time we had gone skiing together. Inside were quite a few women, but none of them had long brown hair like the one I had seen outside. Perhaps I had gotten her hair color wrong.

"This is Riley, Candy, and Carmen. Carmen and I got married a few months ago."

"Well, congratulations," I told him as I said hello to the women.

"You remember Savannah?"

"Holy smokes! She has grown up a lot," I commented, and she grinned, then returned to mixing something in a bowl.

"How do you know Tim?" Carmen asked as she came to my side.

"We used to ski together," I replied.

"Emily and I used to hang out with him and Eve." He paused. "Did you and Eve get married? Is she here?"

I clenched my jaw. "No, that didn't work out."

"I'm sorry to hear that."

"I'd prefer not to think about it," I told him.

"You have a few minutes? I want to introduce you to the rest of the group. They are down in the pool room. Tripp is there, too. He'll be happy to see you. You are not going to believe how old he looks now. He's got his damn license."

"Oh man, watch out," I joked with him as we turned from the kitchen, and I glanced once more around the room—sure now that the woman I saw wasn't one of them and figured she was in the other area with the men.

We talked more as we went, and I told Tim about my day out skiing. "We are supposed to get another good dump of snow later this week."

"Great. I know we want to hit the slopes tomorrow, but we have some gear we need to get sorted out."

"How many people are here?"

"Fourteen of us, but not everyone is skiing. Silvia is not a fan, and Carmen will stay off skis. She's two months pregnant, and we lost the last baby, so she doesn't want to take any chances with this one," he said as we walked down the hallway.

"Oh, man, I'm sorry to hear that. I'm glad she is taking it easy, though."

"Yeah, me too," he replied as we entered the pool room. The eighty-inch television was playing a football game quietly in the background, and my eyes scanned the room to see that there were no women in there. However, I did see Tripp.

"Jesus, you weren't kidding. He's almost a man now."

"Sixteen, about to turn seventeen," Tim told me as Tripp approached to shake my hand.

"Wow, I haven't seen you in years," Tripp said.

"You've grown up. You're making me feel old," I joked.

"I have a car, a job, and a girlfriend now," he said with a wide smile.

"Oh, man, watch out," I laughed.

Tim introduced me to Ethan and Mike as Evan came to join us and explained who was connected to whom.

"Is that everyone?" I asked.

"Uh, yeah," he said, then shook his head as if something had just occurred to him as an afterthought. "No, Coral is here too, but she's upstairs taking a shower, I think."

"And who is she here with?" I asked, not that it mattered.

"No one. She's the only single female in the house besides Savannah," Tim replied and then grinned. "Why? Do you want me to hook you up with her? I'm not sure she's your type."

"I didn't know I had a type," I replied as Ethan handed me a beer.

"Oh, you have a type, and it's usually high-maintenance." He laughed loudly. "And that's definitely not Coral."

I laughed. "Okay, so maybe I do have a type, but thank you, I don't need you to introduce me. I noticed someone standing by the water earlier and didn't think I was introduced to her yet."

"No, she's hiding, but that's Coral. She is one of the reasons we are all out here. She's a big skier, or she used to be, and she works her ass off now and never takes time off. We chipped in and decided to send her on vacation here, on my recommendation, and then we decided to make it a family holiday. Alaina flew us all out here."

"The perks of having a private plane. I keep asking my father to buy one, but he says he likes flying with normal people."

Tim smirked as Evan replied, "It has its perks."

I hung out with them for a little while, and then my mother popped her head into the room and said she was heading back. I finished my beer quickly and told her I'd go with her.

"You don't have to. You can stay."

"No, that's okay. I'm sure I will see them later. I don't want you walking on the slick pathway by yourself," I replied to my mother.

She rolled her eyes playfully, and Tim and Evan walked us to the door. "Please let us know if you need anything here."

"We will," Evan assured her. "Your home is beautiful. Thank you for allowing us to stay here."

I laughed. "If you think the guesthouse is nice, you must see the main house."

Tim laughed. "Holy shit, I didn't even put two and two together. When I came here, I thought it looked familiar, but I didn't even notice your house over there. How I could miss that monstrosity, I don't know."

"You will have to come over and say hello," my mother said. "All the kids are here for Thanksgiving, and we are celebrating

Landan's fortieth birthday." Her face suddenly lit up. "You guys should come for the party on Friday."

"I wouldn't miss that for the world," Tim said as he patted my shoulder.

My mother and I said our goodbyes, and then we took our time going down the steps as it was icing up outside. A few snowflakes fell, but heavy snow wasn't called for tonight. As we began to walk back toward our house, I glanced up at the last balcony and saw the woman from the water standing there.

She was staring at the water but must have heard us because she glanced down. I smiled up at her and waved. She barely raised her hand from the railing in a vague returned hand gesture. There was no smile on her lips. It was too dark to see the details, but I was pretty sure the look on her face wasn't one of happiness.

As I continued to help my mother over the slick ground, I found myself frowning. I didn't want the woman to be unhappy. It was almost impossible to feel that way when you were in Lake Tahoe.

CHAPTER FIVE

CORAL

As much as I wanted to hang around everyone, I also didn't. I ended up eating a little bit and then headed back upstairs. Even though I had taken a long nap on the plane, I was still exhausted. I planned to shower, climb in bed, watch television for a little while, and then go to sleep.

Only, after my shower I found myself back on the balcony. As I stood there, I saw movement below and watched a man and woman walk from the front door to the pathway to the other house.

The man was tall and had darker hair, but I couldn't see much else about him as it was dark now. He saw me and lifted a hand to wave. Who was he? What were they doing here? I gave a brief wave and then watched them until they disappeared around the house.

I shivered in the cold and pulled my jacket tighter to me. A few minutes later, I returned to my room, discarded my coat, and climbed under the covers as I turned on the television. I flipped through a few channels and settled on a movie I loved to watch that had just started.

A short while later, there was a knock on the door, and Silvia poked her head in. "I wasn't sure if you'd be awake."

"I am. You can come in. Did you need something?"

"No, dear, I was just checking on you." She approached the bed, glancing at the television. "Ah, *City of Angels*. I love that movie."

"Yeah, it's one of my favorites too."

"Mind if I join you?" She pointed at the empty side of the bed.

"You don't want to hang around with everyone else?"

"They are a rambunctious group." She laughed. "I'd prefer some quiet after a long day of travel."

I grinned. "Then climb on up." I was happy to have the company and completely understood how she felt.

We talked a little about the movie as she got settled, and then we grew quiet as we watched. A few minutes later, my eyes grew heavy, and I couldn't help but close them and drift off.

When I woke, the television was off, and I was alone. I glanced at my phone to see it was four in the morning, but to me, it was seven. I stretched, happy that I had gotten a decent night's sleep.

I grabbed a sweatshirt to throw over my pajamas, slipped on thick socks, and entered the hallway. The house was dark and silent, and I made my way down to the kitchen. I hadn't looked around the house much, but as I went down, I peeked into open doors and looked around. Eventually, I was in the kitchen and turned on the lights. On the far side of the kitchen was the coffee maker, and I made my way toward it.

I peeked into cabinets and finally found coffee. It was a local brand I'd never had before, and I opened the bag and deeply sniffed. Not bad, I thought as I filled the filter basket and then added water. As the coffee began to brew, I moved around the kitchen more, seeing what else was there. It was stocked with every appliance you could need and then some.

I stood at the window, staring out in the darkness, and knew that once the coffee was done, I would pour myself a cup and find a blanket so I could sit outside.

Ten minutes later, I curled up on a cushioned chair on the front porch. There was also a gas firepit there, and as much as I wished it was on, I had no clue how to turn it on. Steam drifted off the cup into my face, and I inhaled the rich aroma of the coffee before sipping it.

I loved the silence until it was broken by the sound of something running. Was it an animal? It sounded too loud to be an animal, and I watched the corner of the house, wondering if I should be preparing to run inside.

Luckily, it wasn't a wild animal, but I was still slightly alarmed when I noticed it looked like a man running. I leaned back in my seat, hoping he didn't see me, but as he began to run down the path about twenty feet away, he glanced my way and then slowed.

"Hey, sorry to bother you," he said as he stopped, plumes of smoke vaporizing before him from his heavy breathing.

"You're not bothering me, but why are you running? Is something chasing you?"

He stepped a little closer. "No." He laughed slightly. "I like to run in the morning if we don't get much snow. It's safest to run through the plowed areas. I live next door." He came closer and pointed over his shoulder, and I realized it was the man I had seen the night before.

"Hello," I replied. "You were the one leaving last night. I saw you from the balcony."

He nodded and stepped close enough that I could see his face. He was handsome, and his hair was longer in the back and slightly curly. "Yeah, I saw you up there. Great view from there. That room has the best one."

"I don't think there is a window in the house with a bad view."

He chuckled, the sound smooth and mellow, warming me like the warm cup in my hands. "That is true." He paused. "I'm Landan Lancaster."

"Coral Winston," I replied. "You live next door?"

"It's my parents' house, but my family owns this one, too."

"Wow! Two houses on the lake," I commented, thinking he comes from money like Alaina. There is no way a person could afford this kind of house otherwise.

"Yeah, one of the best locations, too."

"I am sure it is." I shivered as I pulled the blanket closer. "I look forward to seeing more of it."

"Are you cold? Why don't you turn the firepit on?"

"I thought about it but realized I didn't know how it worked."

"I can show you."

"Can you?"

"Sure." He nodded, climbed the steps, and walked around the back of the chair I was sitting in. He glanced at me and smiled.

I watched as he reached under the table and turned his hand. "The gas tank is under here; just open the side door. Once the gas is on, the switch is on this side." He flipped the switch, and the flame came to life. Instantaneously, I could feel the heat of the fire.

"That was easy," I commented.

"Yeah, it is pretty easy." He stood up and studied me. "You're up early."

"I'm used to being up around three for work."

"What do you do?" he asked as he took a seat across from me.

"I own a coffee shop, and I have to be there around four to prepare it to open at five."

"A coffee shop? That's great! You can't go wrong with that."

I scoffed, "You might think that."

He cocked his head. "I guess." He glanced at my coffee cup.

"Would you like a cup?"

He studied me for a moment. "Another time, Coral. I need to get my run in and then cook breakfast for the crew. We are hitting the slopes again today."

"You have a lot of friends here?"

"Friends? No, my parents are here, along with my seven siblings."

"Seven." I laughed. "Wow, you have more than I do. I have five."

"I met most of them last night." He started to walk backward. "You guys hitting the slopes today?"

"Yeah, last I heard, we are heading to Heavenly since they have so many different runs."

"You any good?"

I smirked, lifting my chin. "I can hold my own with the best of them."

He nodded, grinning toward me. "Maybe I'll see you out there."

"Maybe you will."

His smile grew. "Nice meeting you, Coral. I'm sure we will see each other again."

"I'm sure we will," I replied, and then he turned and jogged down the stairs, glancing my way and waving before he began to pick up speed and ran toward the lake down a path. "At least I hope we do," I said softly as he disappeared around a gathering of trees.

I thought about him after he left. It had been a while since I met a man who captured my attention. He was very handsome, and I liked his athletic appearance. Not only did he ski, but he was out running and then planned on going out on the slopes. That was a lot of legwork.

Maybe he was one of those guys who went up the slopes and

spent most of his time at the lodge at the top, throwing back beers and joking with his buddies. He'd do a run or two and then call it a day, enjoying the après ski available at the base camp.

I sat there for a while, wondering if he'd come back this way, but after about thirty minutes, I didn't see him again and went to refill my coffee mug. Evan and Alaina were in the kitchen.

"There you are. I was wondering who made the coffee."

I laughed. "Who do you think made the coffee? I've been sitting on the front porch."

"Isn't it a little cold to be sitting out there?"

"No, I had a blanket and turned on the firepit."

"Really? Is it still on?"

"Yeah, I was gonna fill my mug and go back out."

"I'll come with you," he said and glanced at Alaina sitting at the table with her laptop. "She's got some work to do."

We filled our mugs and headed back outside. "I can't believe how nice it is here."

"It is," I stated as I covered myself again.

"You missed meeting a few of the neighbors last night."

"Landan?"

His brow furrowed. "Yeah, how did you know that?"

"I met him this morning. He was out running. He's the one who showed me how to work the firepit."

"Oh, cool. Would you believe not only does his family know Alaina, but he knows Tim too."

"Really? I'm not surprised that he knows Alaina. Everyone seems to know her."

"Yeah, that's how she found this place. They own both houses."

"They must come from a lot of money. I can't imagine owning this one, much less another one."

"Yeah, Alaina said they are big into real estate developments."

I nodded. That made sense.

"Landan is here celebrating Thanksgiving and his birthday with his family."

"He said he has seven siblings."

"How long did you talk to the guy?"

"Just a few minutes."

"Long enough to know his family owns the house, and he has seven siblings. What else did you guys talk about?"

"Why? You are acting like I'm not allowed to talk to someone else," I said defensively.

"No, I was just wondering, that's all."

I looked away from him and stared out over the lake. The sun was rising, and the beauty of the lake was coming to life. God, I loved it here and had barely seen any of the place.

"He seems nice," he stated, and I sipped my coffee, not wanting to discuss Landan anymore.

"What time are we leaving?"

"I think we are planning on heading out around seven-thirty."

"Okay, then I'm going to go in and make breakfast and then get ready."

"Coral, are you okay?"

"I'm fine. Why would you ask?"

"Because you seem so quiet. You didn't hang out with us last night and just don't seem like yourself."

"I'm fine, Evan. I was tired last night."

"You know you can talk to me."

"We are talking," I told him and got to my feet.

"You know that's not what I meant. If something is bothering you, you can tell me."

Should I tell him I felt like an outcast in my family? I didn't think he'd understand, so I said something else. "I'll see you inside."

No one in my family would understand how much of a

failure I felt compared to all of them. I didn't want to think about it. Right now, I wanted to cook breakfast, and then I wanted to lose myself in the rush of the wind and the powder on the slopes.

CHAPTER SIX

LANDAN

W e all got up early and headed out. We decided to hit Heavenly today, which had been my idea. The thought that I might run into Coral somewhere on the mountain was on my mind. It was a massive mountain with the tallest slopes in the area, and the chances of seeing her were slim, but there was a chance.

As I continued my run earlier, I thought about the quiet woman I had seen on the deck. She was pretty, although not the type of woman I usually found interesting. Her voice had been soft but firm, and her eyes had watched me as if she were wondering something. What was it that she saw when she looked at me?

Even though I had initially planned to get breakfast ready, we decided to stop at one of our favorite breakfast spots in the Heavenly Village to get breakfast crepes. It was a small place, but we all loved it there. After eating, we gathered our stuff from the cars and then went to the gondola. It took twenty minutes to ride to the first stop, where we climbed off and discussed which slopes we wanted to run. I intended to work my way up to Skyline Trail, and to do that I needed to get up to Tamarack Lodge.

We split up when we got off at Tamarack Lodge, and Luna, Lance, and Lucas came with me. We were about to get on the Tamarack Express when Tim called my name.

"Hey, man! I didn't expect to see you guys," I said as he approached us. Beside him was his son Tripp. "You the only two up here?"

"No, Coral is here. You didn't meet her last night. She's using the restroom before we head up."

"I met her this morning. Where are you going?"

"Skyline." He grinned. "What did you expect?"

I laughed. "Nothing like starting at the top. You sure you're ready for that?"

"Absolutely."

I glanced around. "Is Coral strong enough of a skier to do the Skyline?"

He chuckled. "I don't think she will have a problem. When did you meet her?"

"She was sitting outside when I went out running this morning."

"Ah, you're still doing that shit." He laughed.

"Yep, every day I can."

Just then, Coral joined us, and I took in the gear she had with her—all-new, top-of-the-line skis and boots, along with a great helmet and goggles. She looked the part, but could she do the part without getting herself killed?

"Hi, Coral," I said as I grinned her way.

She smiled back, almost shyly. "Landan. It's nice to see you again."

"I hear you are heading up to Skyline."

"I guess that is where we are going. Tim said to follow him."

"Well, we are heading there too, so why don't you guys join us."

"Sounds great," Tim said.

Tim and I chatted as we went to the Tamarack Express that would take us to the California Trail. From there, we would ski down to the north of Maggie's Canyon, and then we could take the Sky Express up to the Skyline. It was over ten thousand feet up and gave you the best view of the lake.

Tim chatted easily with my brothers and sister, and I spoke with Tripp on and off as we made our way up. Coral stood off to the side, staring out the window, seemingly at peace with the view.

Occasionally, she would glance my way, and I pretended I didn't notice. Once, I turned to her, and she looked away quickly and began to blush as she put her back to me.

I stepped away from Tripp and stood close to her, pointing to something in the distance. "The house is over there. You can barely make it out."

She followed where I pointed and smiled. "It looks so small, but it is anything but."

The gondola shifted, and I lost my balance slightly, leaning into her momentarily. "Sorry." She looked my way, and our eyes locked. She had pretty blue eyes, even though there were circles under them. "How many times have you gone skiing?"

She blinked and quickly looked away. "Quite a few times."

"And you've done diamond slopes before?"

She scoffed, "You don't have to worry about me. I can take care of myself, Landan."

"I'm not worried. I just want to make sure you aren't biting off more than you can chew."

She turned to look at me, raising a brow. "I am sure I can give you a run for your money."

I chuckled as she glanced away. I leaned forward, my cheek touching hers as the gondola shifted again. "I look forward to it, Coral."

She turned her face, and our lips almost brushed. I shifted

back at her surprised expression, and she peered at my mouth. "Why would you look forward to it?"

I shrugged and leaned back against the pole behind me. "Because I love to ski and enjoy doing it with others who can keep up."

"I can keep up, Landan. Don't worry about that."

"Alright, then. I look forward to it." Shortly after that, we got off and shifted to the side to prepare our skis.

"We're doing the California Trail to Maggie's Canyon?" Tim asked.

"Yeah, that's the plan. Then we can take the express up."

"Perfect." He turned to Coral. "Just wait till you see the view from up there."

"Lead the way," she said happily. Her attitude seemed lighter now than it was earlier.

Skis were on, binding checked, poles ready, and the helmets tightened with the goggles in place. As I looked over at Coral, I had to admit that she looked cute as hell.

Lucas and Luna were the first to take off. Behind them, Tim and Tripp headed down, and I watched Coral, prepared to follow her in case she needed help. If she weren't up for it, I'd help direct her to a safer slope once we got down the trail. Lance was set to follow up the rear. I watched as Coral shifted through the soft snow and began to descend. She moved back and forth as if she were testing her skis, and just as I started, she rotated her hips, legs, and skis and took off.

I chuckled as I followed her and heard Lance laugh louder. Coral zipped down, turning deftly as if she were born on skis. Damn, I thought as I grinned. A woman after my own heart, and that thought almost made me stumble.

I watched her and kept my eye on the trail. She flew past Tim and Tripp, and I lowered my center of gravity and caught up to her. She was outstanding, and she glanced back at me once, grinning.

Another thirty feet down, and she slid to a fast stop. One that I had not expected, and I almost plowed over her, but at the last moment, I turned and went around her. Somehow, I didn't fall and stopped twenty feet away.

She was staring out at the lake, her face filled with an expression that I hadn't seen in a long time and one I understood so well. The view enthralled her. I waited as Tim and Trip zoomed past us, and then Lance threw a curtain of snow at me with a laugh as he went around me.

"Ass!" I yelled after him playfully and glanced back to see Coral slowly sliding my way.

"You didn't have to stop."

"I know, but skiing with a partner is safer."

"Yeah, I know."

"You are pretty good."

"I did a lot of skiing when I was younger." She looked back out at the lake. "I can't get over how incredible it is."

I turned to her, staring at her profile. "Yeah, I know." I told myself I'm talking about the lake's view, not her.

She peered my way. "How often do you ski?"

"As often as I can."

She nodded. "I guess we should get moving."

"I can show you some of my favorite slopes if you want. They aren't all here at Heavenly."

She studied me. "I'd like that, Landan."

Yeah, I would, too, I thought as I stared back at her. This crazy urge to lean forward and kiss her filled me. I cleared my throat and looked away. "We should get going. They are going to think we crashed."

"Okay," she said, adjusting her goggles back before nodding at me. With a quick twist, she was moving again, and I grinned as I put my goggles back on and followed.

She was incredible, and I loved every minute of watching her. From time to time, she would slow, and I knew she was spending as much time looking at the scenery of the lake as she was at the slopes.

Everyone was waiting for us at the bottom, and Coral stopped with a laugh. "God, this feels good."

Tim chuckled as Luna replied, "Finally, another girl who skis as well as we do!"

We headed toward the express lift to get us up to the Skyline, and once we were on, I made sure to stand near Coral. Her eyes were glued out the window, and I pointed out things as we went up. Tripp stood on her other side, asking questions about places as we went.

At the top, we all stood quietly, looking over the lake.

"I can't believe a place like this exists," Coral said so softly that I barely heard her over the wind.

"I know," I said as I moved closer to her. "It's like you are in heaven."

She blinked quickly and glanced up. The words that left her lips shocked me. "Hi, Mom."

I frowned. "Your mother has passed?"

She nodded. "Yeah, she died a few years ago."

"I'm so sorry, Coral."

"Thanks." She paused and looked around. "Would it be weird to say that I almost feel closer to her here? She would have loved this. She liked to ski, too."

"No, not weird at all. I'm sorry she's not here to enjoy it with you."

She grinned up at the sky. "She's here. I can feel her."

I gave her a tender smile, and then we followed the group, preparing to head down. Lance went ahead this time with the rest of the group, and Coral and I took our time, pausing at points to take in the scenery and then speeding up to zoom down the trail around slower skiers.

Halfway down, I realized I missed having someone to ski with. Yeah, I loved going with my friends and siblings, but having someone else who enjoyed stopping along the way and taking a moment to enjoy the world around us was incredible. Not that Eve had done that with me. She liked to ski but could not do the more extensive slopes.

I hoped she meant what she said about letting me show her some other slopes. As we hit the Milky Way, one of the diamond trails that led to more dangerous slopes, I wondered if she'd want to try one of them, but she kept to the main trail, bypassing the gates either open or closed.

I stayed with her, and we'd laugh and play around as we wove in and out. We eventually got down to where the Dipper Express was and took it back up. Coral decided she wanted to head through one of the tree-filled trails, and the others went toward a different trail.

It was just the two of us now, and I stayed a safe distance behind her as we wove between the trees. These were more dangerous trails, and one mistake could be a big one, but we made it through quickly, and it was back at the bottom that I threw my arm around her shoulders with a laugh, giving her a slight hug. "I will ski with you any day."

She grinned at me as I let her go and stepped back so it wasn't weird. "You have no idea how good it feels to be out here. I forgot how much I loved skiing."

"Why did you stop?"

She shrugged and looked away. "Life. I decided that being a ski bum wasn't all I wanted out of life."

"What did you want?" I asked as we made our way toward a small trail that would eventually move us back to the main gondola so we could return to Heavenly Base Camp.

"I wanted to have a coffee shop. My goal was to own one at the ski resort, but I could never afford that, so I opened one in my hometown."

I had a feeling that there was more to it, but I didn't want to push. "You could open a second one."

She laughed. "I'd probably fail at that one too."

I frowned as she skied ahead of me slightly. "Did your current one fail?"

"Not yet, but it is only a matter of time." Before I could say anything else, she spoke again. "Come on, I'm starving!"

CHAPTER SEVEN

CORAL

I hadn't felt this free in years. There was no stress or worries over deliveries or employees—no concerns about paying the bills or figuring out how I would afford the new lease. It was just crisp, clean air sailing past me as I raced down.

After Landan mentioned being close to heaven, I honestly felt my mother was there with me. She was cheering me on and laughing with me as I went. It was like she was beside me, and I treasured every moment.

Of course, having Landan as a companion wasn't bad either. We complemented each other in our skills. He was patient with me as I paused to take in the scenery and seemed just as happy to take it in as I was. That puzzled me since he was a regular here. Could it possibly have kept its amazing appeal to him after so long?

I couldn't imagine ever getting tired of the beauty around me. Having an attractive man with me was a bonus, and from time to time, I would watch him without him knowing what I was doing. He was handsome and kind, funny, and responsive.

He also seemed to pick up on things I said that I didn't necessarily mean for him to pick up on, like my failing business.

I didn't want to talk about it with him. No one needed to know, and I didn't want to ruin our budding friendship. I could imagine him looking down at me or being disappointed that I wasn't a better businessperson. He knew Alaina and probably traveled in the same circles as her. That meant that he was very good at business.

However, that didn't make me want to ditch him. No, I was enjoying our time too much to do that.

We made our way back to the main gondola, and I was exhausted by the time we climbed on to head down. I yawned and tried to hide it behind my gloved fist, but Landan saw it and laughed.

"All the fresh air wore you out."

I nodded. "Yes, it did. I am probably going to hurt like hell tomorrow. It's been a while since I was this physically active."

"I understand. I was hurting a little this morning."

I laughed. "And yet, you brutalized yourself today."

He shrugged a shoulder and laughed. "It was worth it."

"How was it worth it?"

He turned and faced me. "I got to spend it doing what I loved and with someone who appeared to enjoy it as much."

I got lost in his soft brown eyes. "Well, thank you."

"For what?"

"For showing me around up there, and well, for hanging with me. I wasn't really in the mood to be a fifth wheel."

He chuckled. "I understand that. It's hard to be single around so many couples."

"You don't know the half of it," I muttered.

He shifted slightly, glancing at me, then out the window. "So, you're not seeing anyone back home?"

"No, I don't have time to date."

"I know that better than you might think."

"What about you? No girlfriend or wife hiding someplace?"

He laughed briskly. "No, neither of those."

I nodded, happier to hear that than I should have been.

He turned to me. "Would you have dinner with me?"

My face flipped toward his. "Me?"

He looked around at a few other people who were busy in their conversations. "Yes, you. Did you think I was talking to someone else in here?"

"No, I'm just surprised you asked."

"Why would you be surprised?"

I shrugged. "I don't know."

"Well, I would very much like to take you to dinner, Coral."

"I'm not sure what my family has planned tonight."

"It doesn't have to be tonight." He paused, and I felt slightly let down that he was already taking back his offer. "You know, we could go off on our own tomorrow. I could show you a few sights, and we could hit another few slopes. Maybe go over to Squaw Creek or Kirkwood. I was over there yesterday. It was amazing."

"I heard Kirkwood had some good slopes."

He nodded. "They do, but we better wait to see how you feel tomorrow. If you are hurting, it might be smarter to wait a day. They will kick your ass. That's why I am sore from yesterday."

"Okay, well, I'll wait to see how I feel."

"So, what do you say? Do you want to spend the day with me?"

What did I have to lose? It's not like my family would miss me much, and this trip was supposed to be my vacation. "Let me check with the family to make sure they don't have a problem with it."

"Sure," he replied, appearing a bit disappointed that I hadn't said yes right away. He smiled my way and then looked out the window as we descended into the village. We gathered our things, and then I followed him out of the gondola. We looked around outside. "I have no idea where anyone is."

We set our things down and pulled out our phones. He seemed to find something out before I did. "Looks like everyone is at Base Camp Pizza."

"My family, too?"

"Yep, Luna said they were outside at a table waiting for us."

We went to find them and located half of the original group. All of them grinned at me as we joined them. "About time," Carmen said. "We were wondering what you two were up to."

I rolled my eyes at her because I heard the taunt in her voice. So, I was enjoying some time with a handsome man. Was there anything wrong with that? No. "We were having fun skiing."

"Yep, I'm sure that is all it was," Riley tacked on with a snort.

"Did you guys order something? I'm starving," I asked as I took a seat next to Tim.

"No, we were waiting for you guys to come back. Your dad and Silvia returned to the house with Evan and Alaina to get a head start on dinner."

"Oh, well, I need a snack before we head back. I haven't had anything in hours."

"We can grab you something for the ride back," Tim said.

"Or Coral and I can get something to eat here. You guys go," Landan said from behind me. "I'll get her home later."

Tim looked at me carefully. "Do you want to stay?"

I laughed. "Yeah, I can stay with him. It's a good idea. You guys go ahead. I need food as soon as possible."

"You guys mind if I stay?" Luna asked.

"I'm going to stay, too," Lance replied. "But I won't cramp your style. I see a few of my friends over there. Luna, did you see Marcus sitting by the front firepit."

"Where?" She quickly spun around and giggled. "Oh, I'm staying."

"Yeah, anyone who wants to stay can. I have my Expedition. I can take everyone back."

With that decided, Landan and I followed them to the parking lot. I put my gear back into the truck that Tim was driving, removed my ski pants, grabbed my hiking boots, and took my small backpack with my wallet.

"You sure you want to stay?" Tim asked.

"Yeah, why wouldn't I? He's not a creeper, is he?"

He laughed. "Who, Landan?" I nodded. "No, he's one of the nicest guys I know. If he were a creeper, I wouldn't have left you alone with him on the mountain."

"Then you guys go and have a good time. It will be nice to hang out and enjoy the atmosphere."

"Yeah, you go enjoy the après ski."

"It's funny to hear that after so long," I replied. The après ski was the fun after skiing—the drinks by the fires, the laughter with friends. It had been so long since I partook in that kind of thing.

"See you later," I told him after giving him a quick hug and saying goodbye to Tripp and Carmen.

"I think she likes him," I heard my sister say.

Maybe I did, but that had nothing to do with anything. This was my vacation, and if I wanted to have a crush on a guy, I could. It would never go anywhere, but I could enjoy it while I was here.

I found Landan waiting for me at the entrance back to the base camp. "You ready?"

"Yep, lead me to food!"

"I'm starving too. What are you in the mood for?"

"Um, that pizza place looked nice."

"It's the best. Come on," He put his arm around me to lead me that way, and instead of letting him drop it, I slid my arm around his waist. He grinned down at me as if he was happy that I did.

I wasn't going to look a gift horse in the mouth.

When we returned, he asked for a table for two because Lance and Luna had ditched us for their friends who were sitting around a large firepit listening to music.

"I miss this kind of thing."

"Where did you ski?"

"Oh, I've skied at several places, but mostly in the east. We don't have anything as awesome as you have here, but we have some great smaller runs. If you were east, you could do Big Boulder, Camelback, and Jack Frost. South of us is Seven Spring, Blue Knob, and Whitetail." He seemed very interested in what I was saying, so I continued. "I worked at Seven Spring for a while, but it was a little too freestyle, so I moved up to Blue Knob and enjoyed it. It has the highest summit in the state and some of the most difficult terrain."

"What do you mean, you worked there?"

"I was ski patrol and gave lessons occasionally."

He laughed. "No wonder you ski so well."

I grinned. "Yeah, maybe I should have mentioned that earlier."

"I'm glad that you didn't. I enjoyed being surprised."

"As much as I have skied, I've never skied anything like today. It was amazing. It felt so different."

"I guess I am spoiled. I've skied a few other ranges, but nothing compares to here for me. Work generally has me busy, so I don't travel as often as I used to."

"What do you do?"

"I work in real estate like my father. Mostly buying and selling commercial, but I have some vacation homes around."

"Must be nice. Do you visit those vacation homes?"

He laughed. "Not as often as I'd like."

"Do you have anything on the East Coast?"

He shook his head. "No, but maybe I need to invest in something."

"Why would you say that?"

"Because then I'd have an excuse to see you again. You could take me to Blue Knob."

His words warmed me. "I'd like that."

"I would, too." The waitress returned and took our order, and then Landan told me more about the area. I was hooked on his every word and over dinner, our conversation turned to our families.

"How long has your dad been seeing Silvia?"

"Um, since about the time that Carmen and Tim got together, which was in March, I think."

"What do you think of your father seeing someone?"

I shrugged. "As long as he is happy. Silvia is very nice. We get along great. Last night, she curled up in bed with me and watched a movie." I laughed. "Except I fell asleep shortly after it started."

"What movie?"

"*City of Angels.*" He grinned. "What? Do you have something against chick flicks?"

"Not at all. Luna and Laney make me watch them. I laughed because some of *City of Angels* was filmed here in Lake Tahoe."

I jerked back. "Shut up! It was not!"

"It was filmed at Fallen Leaf Lake. *The Bodyguard* movie with Whitney Houston was, too."

"Oh my god! Seriously?"

"Yep."

"That is so cool." Even though I was excited and happy, I still couldn't stop the yawn that attacked me.

"Just imagine how well you will sleep tonight." He chuckled.

"I will probably pass out."

"You and me both."

We enjoyed the rest of dinner, and I yawned more often as the day caught up.

After one of my latest yawns, he said, "We should get you back. Otherwise, you might be too tired to go out tomorrow."

"Yeah, probably a good idea."

He paid the bill and then went to find Lance and Luna, who told us to go ahead without them. They would get a ride later or find someplace to stay for the night. I didn't think Luna would have a problem with that since she was sitting on a man's lap, looking happy as a clam.

"Looks like it is just you and me," Landan said as we began to walk away, and I suddenly felt nervous. I had been with him all day, pretty much by myself. Now that the sun had set and my stomach was full, it felt more personal.

He took my hand as we walked toward the parking lot and glanced at me to check that it was alright. I squeezed his hand to let him know I approved—more than approved.

When we reached his SUV, he opened the door for me, and I was about to step on the running board when I turned to him. "Thank you for today. It has been one of the best days of my life, Landan."

He touched my cheek. "I'm glad, Coral. I have to admit, it's been a pretty fantastic day for me too."

We stared at each other for a few seconds, and then as if by mutual consent, we each stepped forward, and he lowered his face to kiss me. It wasn't a crazy passionate kiss, but it lit sparks in my core.

He winked at me as he pulled away, and I climbed into the SUV, giggling silently. What a vacation this was turning out to be.

8

CHAPTER EIGHT

LANDAN

I wasn't sure what was happening between Coral and me, but I liked it. She was funny and adventurous, and I liked that in a woman. She was an excellent skier, and the look she got on her face when she gazed at the scenery warmed my soul.

Many people came here and stared at the beauty of the lakes and mountains, but few took the time to absorb it. She did, and I loved that. From the moment she had arrived yesterday, she had been drawn to the scenery.

To me, Lake Tahoe was more than a beautiful area. It was my home. The one place on this earth that felt right to me. No matter what else was happening in the world, when I was here, everything righted itself.

I was thrilled she would allow me to show her around the lake, too. Of course, I wanted to get her out on the slopes again, but I also wanted to show her other things. There were many touristy things to do, but most were easier to get to during the warmer months.

"Do you like to hike?" I asked her as we drove home.

"I do, but I haven't done that in a long time."

"Why not?"

"Because I am always working," she said almost sadly.

"You should return in the warmer months, and I can take you hiking. If you think it's beautiful in winter, you should see it in the spring when everything is alive, but there is still snow on the mountains."

"Is there always snow up there?"

"Most of the time, there are a few peaks that keep it year-round, but in the late summer, most of it is gone."

"I can only imagine how beautiful it would look in the summer. Does it get busy around here then?"

"It does. The crowds are coming in right now, and they won't die down until at least April. Then in July and August, it's crazy out here as people enjoy the lake."

"Can you swim in it?"

"Sure, but it's chilly." I grinned at her. "We waterski and tube in the summer."

"You guys have a boat?"

"We do. We have a couple of boats, but they are in storage for the winter. We also paddleboard and kayak."

"I have always wanted to try that," she replied wistfully, and I peered her way. I saw her yawn again and chuckled. "Why are you laughing?"

"Because you're so tired, it's cute."

"Cute?" She laughed. "I am far from cute."

I smirked. Coral was cute, but not only that, she was pretty, too. I had a feeling she'd deny it if I told her that. "If you say so," I finally said.

"What time works for you tomorrow?"

"What time do you think you'll be up?"

"I don't know, probably by five, that's eight at home. I can't remember the last time I slept past six."

"Then you need to do that while you are on vacation."

"Maybe I'll get the chance. What should I bring?"

I thought about that for a moment. "Bring your ski gear, that's for sure, but I'd bring a change of clothes and a bathing suit."

She laughed. "Didn't you just say that the water is too cold?"

"I did, but I wasn't thinking about the lake."

"You know of an inside pool?"

I was considering something more along the lines of some hot springs, but they might be hard to get to. If that didn't work out, I knew a nice hot tub spot. "I'm thinking more of a hot tub."

"Oh, that I could do. I might need to hit the one at the house tonight."

I glanced at her. "You should do that before you go to bed. It will help you sleep."

"I'm not sure I'll have trouble doing that."

We chatted a little more as we drove, and she grew quiet. I glanced her way to see her head back, her eyes closed, and I grinned. She had fallen asleep. I drove the rest of the way home in silence, peering at her occasionally when the road was straight.

I pulled down the driveway to my house, although I should have pulled down the one to the guesthouse. I'd walk her over once I parked. It would be nice to walk her over, and maybe I could get another kiss before I left her on the porch.

I touched her arm. "Coral, we're home."

She opened her eyes, blinking a few times to try and wake up. "I'm sorry. I didn't mean to fall asleep."

"It's okay. You needed it."

"Wait, this is your house, isn't it?"

"Yeah, I'll walk you over to yours so you know where the path is." I climbed out, and she opened the door as I rounded the SUV.

I took her hand as she closed the door, and we began to walk past my house and toward the path that led to the guesthouse.

Halfway there, she stopped, and I glanced back at her. That was when I heard laughter coming from the front porch of the guesthouse.

"I guess they are waiting up for you," I whispered to her.

She shrugged and turned toward the water. "I was hoping they would be in bed. I wanted to take a moment and enjoy the night before I went inside."

I stepped behind her and ran my hands down her arms. She leaned back against me, and I wrapped my arms around her, resting my cheek against the side of her head. We stood quietly for a few moments, enjoying the cold air and the sounds of the night that were interrupted occasionally by laughter.

She sighed. "I guess I should go."

"We could stay here longer."

"I need to get some sleep if you are going to show me around tomorrow. Falling asleep on you once was enough." She chuckled softly.

I brushed my lips against her head. "I enjoyed having you sleep beside me." I wished I had been lying beside her while she did, but it had been nice how it happened.

"That's funny," she said with a giggle. She stepped forward, and my arms dropped as she turned toward me. "What time did you say?"

"Five forty-five okay with you? If you want to go someplace and watch the sunrise, that is."

"Yes, please," she replied as she lifted her face.

I couldn't hold off anymore and cupped her cheek, leaning down to kiss her. This time, I didn't pull away right away, and Coral stepped closer to me, placing her hands on my chest. I curled one arm around her, and her arms wound around my neck as the kiss deepened.

Finally, we began pulling back and stared at one another. I could have kept kissing her, but it was probably better that we stopped. "Let's get you to your house."

"I should go alone. I don't need them all asking questions."

"You sure? I don't mind walking you over."

"No, I'll be fine. The path is well lit."

"Okay, then I'll see you at five forty-five."

"I'll see you in the morning," Neither of us moved.

"Are you going to tell them you are going out with me?"

She shrugged. "Maybe, but probably not."

I laughed. "You embarrassed to be seen with me?"

"No." She shook her head and leaned forward. "I want to keep you all to myself. If I told other people you were taking me on an adventure, they might want to come."

I tapped my finger on her nose. "Then don't you tell a soul. I want you all to myself tomorrow."

Her smile grew, and her eyes sparkled in the darkness. "I'd like that."

I kissed her gently one more time. "Sleep well, Coral. I'll see you in the morning."

"Night, Landan, and thank you."

"It was my pleasure."

I watched as she started down the path and waited until she disappeared around the corner of the house before I returned to mine. It had been a while since I looked forward to spending time with someone who wasn't in my family.

When I got inside, my mother was sitting in the living room before the fire. "Are you alone?"

"I brought Coral home, but Lance and Luna are still at base camp."

"Coral?"

"Yes, she was upstairs when we were over there last night."

"Is she the one you were skiing with all day?"

"Yeah, how do you know?"

"Lucas told me. He said she was a good skier, and you two took off alone."

"We did."

61

"Is she nice?"

I grinned as I leaned back on the couch. "Yeah, she's really nice."

My mother was quiet for a few seconds. "It's good to see you smile like that again."

"Like what?"

"Like you are alive and interested in living again."

"Come on, Mom, I've always lived."

"Yes, but you did most things alone or with your brothers. I'm glad that you met this young woman."

"I'm taking her out tomorrow to show her parts of the lake."

"You are, but what about her family?"

"I have a feeling she wants some space from her family."

"Well, we understand how difficult it can be around large families, don't we?"

I laughed. "Yes, we do."

"I hope you two have a nice time. Just remember something, Landan."

"What's that, Mom?"

"She's not from around here, and she has a life where she lives."

I frowned. "I know that, Mom. I'm just showing her a good time."

"Okay, I just didn't want you to get too enamored with her, and then she leaves and breaks your heart."

I laughed and stood. "Not going to happen, Mom." I kissed her brow. "I'm heading up. I want to take a hot shower. We are leaving early, so don't expect me here for breakfast."

"Sleep well, honey."

"Love you, Mom."

"Love you too, Landan."

I stopped in the kitchen, grabbed a bottle of water, and headed up to my room. I stood under the water in the shower and thought about my day with Coral. As I dwelled over the kiss we'd shared as we said goodbye, I felt my body responding. I quickly flipped the hot water to cold and tensed as it washed over me.

"Gah," I groaned, but that did it, and I turned off the water and stepped out, grabbing a towel. I didn't want to get ahead of myself.

I thought about going back downstairs, but I climbed into bed instead. I was almost as tired as Coral was, and if we were to have a good day, I needed to get some rest.

I set my phone on the charger and turned off the light. I thought about skiing with Coral today and smiled as I drifted off to sleep.

The following day, I was up early, and I went downstairs and packed a breakfast picnic, along with a thermos of coffee. I had left my ski gear in the Expedition, so I went out to make sure it was there and threw in some things we might need today, like snowshoes and a couple of warm blankets.

I turned when I heard something outside the garage and hit the door button. Coral was setting stuff on the ground, and I eyed the pile. "Good morning!"

"Morning." She grinned. "I hope I got everything."

I eyed the large pile of ski gear and the two bags she had with her. "Did you leave anything in your room?"

She laughed. "Yes, of course. You said to bring another outfit, and I wasn't sure if that meant for indoor or outdoor, so I packed both—plus a swimsuit."

"Perfect," I replied, and we began to pack the truck.

"Where are we off to?" she asked as I closed the back hatch.

I stepped before her, smiling down into her bright-blue eyes. She looked a lot more rested today. "First, we will watch the sunrise and have a light breakfast picnic. How does that sound?"

"Did you bring coffee?"

I snorted. "Of course, I brought coffee. Can you even watch the sunrise without it?"

She sighed. "A man after my own heart."

I laughed at what she said but remembered that I had said something similar about her yesterday while we were skiing.

I quickly stepped away from her before I could say or do something stupid.

CHAPTER NINE

CORAL

"Where are we going to watch the sunrise?"

I pulled onto the main road. "The best place to see it: Emerald Bay. It's the most photographed place here in Lake Tahoe."

"I think I read that someplace," I said.

"How did it go when you got back last night?"

"Fine." I shrugged. "They asked lots of questions, but otherwise they were fine."

"What kind of questions?"

"Like, did I have fun? What did we do? Did I like you, those kinds of things."

"Yeah." He peered at me. "What did you tell them?"

I frowned at him. "You already know what we did."

"I meant about liking me." He grinned my way.

I laughed easily. "I'm here, aren't I?"

"Well, that's good to know. I thought maybe you only came with me so you could get away from your family."

"Oh, that's the real reason. I didn't want to offend you," I joked back at him and hiked a brow in question. "I'm kidding. I do like you, Landan."

"I'm glad because I like you too, Coral."

"Okay, so we have that determined. We like one another. Great!"

We both laughed, and I found I liked her morning humor. She didn't appear to be one of those women who were grumpy in the morning. Or perhaps she had been up for hours and had already consumed three cups of coffee.

"What are we doing after we watch the sunrise?"

"Well, I'm not sure. Let's see how things go. How are you feeling today?"

"Admittedly, a bit sore. I was too tired to get in the hot tub last night and opted for a long shower."

"I did the same," he replied. "You sleep well? You look rested."

"I slept like a baby," I told him, and I had. I couldn't remember the last time I slept that well. "My alarm had to wake me up."

"What time did you get up?"

"About forty minutes ago."

His face snapped toward mine, and he looked me over. "No way you got ready in thirty minutes."

I snickered as I replied, "I most certainly did. I'm not one to take a long time getting ready. I don't wear much makeup; I just had to brush my hair and pull it back after getting dressed." I shrugged, thinking that probably wasn't his type, but that was me.

"Well, you look damn good for just brushing your hair. Most women would kill to have a complexion as smooth as yours without makeup."

"Yeah, and how much do you know about complexions?" I joked.

"I have three sisters, and one has a skincare line." He rolled his eyes. "And she made me try all her products for her men's line."

I laughed loudly. "I bet that was fun."

"Some of it wasn't that bad, but there were a few things that I refused to use."

"Like what?"

"Like nose hair conditioner," he stated, and I burst out laughing.

"You have got to be kidding me."

"No. I refused to use it. Nose hair should not be conditioned."

As we drove, we talked more about silly things like that, and before I knew it, we were pulling off the road onto the shoulder. "Are we there?"

"We are," he stated and looked behind him before he opened the door. "Be careful. It might be slippery on that side."

I stepped out cautiously, and he was right, but I managed to keep on my feet and not slip under the car.

He handed me two blankets. "You carry one of these, and I'll take the other one and the bag." He threw a backpack over his shoulder and closed the hatch as another car came past and began to pull over on the shoulder.

He took my hand, and we crossed the street as another car approached. That one didn't stop, and I carefully watched my footing as I followed Landan. He pulled a flashlight out of his pocket and lit the pathway, which was helpful.

He paused by a guardrail and then stepped over. "Where are you going?"

"Come on, I know a great place, but we must climb about ten feet."

I looked around us. "Are we allowed to do this?"

He grinned in the brightening morning. "I won't tell if you don't."

Oh, we were going to break the law, awesome! "What a way to start the adventure," I said, straddling the guardrail and climbing over.

"Just wait," he commented as he held my arm to make sure I didn't fall. "Now, hug the wall here and step carefully. It will be slippery, but it shouldn't be too bad."

I followed behind him, and he would take a few steps, then shine the light behind him so I could follow his steps. We made it down the incline, and I only slipped once. Once we got to the main section, it flattened out, and he took my hand and pulled me along some rocks. We came to a small overhang of rocks, and below the overhang was a large flat boulder. He set the backpack down and unfolded one of the blankets, "Here we are."

I looked around. "This is very cool."

"Wait till the sun comes up." He glanced over his shoulder. "In about fifteen minutes, that sky over there is going to be amazing."

"Alright, it better be," I told him and helped him spread the blanket over the rock. It was a thick cushioned blanket, and after he put that one out, he took the other one and set it aside, then put his hands on my hips.

"What are you doing?"

"I'm going to lift you."

I couldn't help but grin, and without any trouble, he had me in the air and was putting me on the rock. "Aren't you strong," I commented.

"I ate my Wheaties today."

I chuckled again and realized that I had been laughing a lot since I'd met him. God, it felt good to laugh again. As he climbed beside me, I had a moment of guilt for being here and enjoying myself while my business was tanking back east, but the moment he settled beside me and began to cover our laps, I shoved the guilt aside.

He put the backpack between us and removed Tervis mugs and a thermos. He also took out a container that he said had muffins in it and another one with fruit.

"It's not fancy, but it will hold us over until we can get a better breakfast."

"It's perfect," I replied because, quite honestly, it was.

"Aw, shit," he muttered as he stared into the bag.

"What? Did you forget something?"

"I forgot to put cream and sugar into the bag for your coffee."

I pushed his shoulder. "Oh my god! Forget it. The date is over. I want to go home." He stared at me, and I laughed loudly. "I'm kidding. You will be happy to hear that I drink most coffee black."

He stared at me. "You do? You aren't just saying that?"

I shook my head. "Nope, I prefer it black. Sometimes I will sweeten it in the afternoon and add oat milk, but in the morning, it's always black coffee."

He stared at me. "That's how I drink it."

"See, something else we have in common." I held up the mugs while he poured the coffee into them.

"I am beginning to believe we have a lot in common, Coral."

"Perhaps we do," I said before sticking my nose over the cup and inhaling.

"What are you doing?"

"Breathing the coffee."

"Breathing the coffee?" He snickered. "Is that even a thing?"

"It is if you are a coffee snob."

"I enjoy coffee but can't say I'm a snob. What kind of coffee do you serve in your café?"

"Um, it's a local roast. I am sure you have never heard of it."

"What is the name? I do travel around, so you never know. I'm sure I probably saw it someplace."

"Nope, this is only available in my café."

"An exclusive?" I nodded. "How did you manage that?"

"I sourced the beans, and—"

"And what?"

I sighed. "And I'm the one who roasts them. That's why I get to work so early. I do a batch when I get in, but I have to watch them carefully. My roasting machine is very temperamental. If they go even a minute too long, they are ruined and they are expensive."

"Where do you get the beans?"

"I have them imported from Costa Rica."

"Wow, that's impressive. I bet you do good business."

I stared at the horizon where the outline of the mountains was starting to come into view. "Look, you can see the mountains." I redirected his attention away from my company.

"I told you it would be up soon."

"How did you find this place?"

"A friend of mine brought me here. He used to bring girls here all the time."

"Oh, really? And how many have you brought here?"

"Only one, and she didn't appreciate it."

I glanced around. How could you not appreciate this? It was a romantic spot, and the company was incredible. "Well, I am sorry for their loss, but I can assure you that I already appreciate this view. Is that water down there?"

"Yep, that's the famous Emerald Bay. A castle is below us, down on the lake's edge."

"A castle? Like a real castle?"

"Yep, it's the Vikingsholm Castle. It was built in 1929 by a woman from Chicago who relocated here after her husband died. It was designed using some of the finest Scandinavian architecture."

"A castle? A real-life castle?"

"Yep." He nodded. "I would take you down to see it, but it is closed during the winter. You'd have to come back and visit me in the summer."

"I might have to do that just to see a real-life castle. How do you know so much about it? Do you have an interest in architecture?"

"At one point, I thought of being an architect, but my father pushed me to follow in his footsteps. Occasionally, I read about it, and I am interested."

"Are you disappointed you didn't do what you originally wanted?"

He shook his head and leaned back on his elbow. "No. Now I enjoy it as a hobby. What about you? You ever think about doing anything other than owning a café?"

I laughed. "Yeah, pretty much every day."

"Why? You don't like it?"

"No, it's not that." I sighed as I stared out over the lightening sky, and the first glimpses of golden yellows and oranges began to fill the sky. "I'm afraid that my business is going to fail. I've had some issues, and I'm not sure I can rebound from them."

"What are the issues? Maybe I can help."

"Thanks, but I'd prefer not to dwell on them. I'll figure something out," I grinned widely at him. "I always do."

He studied my face. "Okay, I get the impression that you don't want to discuss it, so I'll let it go."

"Thank you, Landan."

He touched my hand. "But if you want to discuss it, I'm willing to listen."

"Thank you. I do appreciate that." I turned back to the view. "Wow, would you look at that."

"Oh, I'm seeing it," he said softly, and I glanced back at him. He winked at me and diverted his attention toward the sky.

The sky only got more incredible, and after a while, I shivered. "Do you want to go?"

"Are you kidding me? I never want to leave," I said.

He shifted around on the rock and came to sit behind me, putting his legs on either side of me. "You can lean on me. I'm back far enough to have the wall behind me for support."

I cozied up to him, welcoming the heat of his body and the closeness. God, I missed having someone close to me. How long had it been? Five? Six years?

He wrapped his arms around me, and we stayed like that, watching the sun rise until it was above the mountains, and then I looked over my shoulder. "Thank you, Landan. That might have been the most beautiful sunrise I have ever seen."

He leaned forward and kissed me. "I'm glad you enjoyed it."

I ran my hand down his neck, pulling him forward again as I shifted to the side so he could kiss me again. After a few moments, I began to turn to get closer to him, and before I realized it, I was sitting on his lap, and the two of us were making out like we were teenagers.

CHAPTER TEN

LANDAN

I hadn't expected this, but I wouldn't stop it anytime soon. Something about Coral filled a piece of me that had been empty for a long time.

She was passionate, not just in her kisses but in how she looked at the world around her.

The kissing intensified, and I ran my hands over her thick coat, wishing it was a warm summer morning so we didn't have as many clothes on. Her mind must have been in the same thought pattern because she reached between us and unzipped my jacket so she could touch my chest.

I quickly unzipped her coat and ran my hands up her back. She arched toward me, and I ran my lips down her throat, loving the natural taste of her skin. I skimmed my hands around the sides of her breasts, and she whimpered slightly.

This woman was driving me wild, and I couldn't help myself as I lifted her shirt and cupped her breast. I wasn't sure if it was the excitement or the cold air, but her nipples were hard and erect, just like my cock. I thumbed her nipple over her bra, and she whimpered again.

I peeled the material off her breast and dropped my mouth

to it, sucking it in and twirling my tongue around the peak. She held my head there, her fingers laced through my hair. If it were warmer, I would have continued to undress her and make love to her right here, but that wouldn't happen.

I pulled back, gazing into her bright eyes. The beautiful sunrise behind her only made the image that much better. "I can't remember the last time I wanted a woman as much as I want you right now, Coral."

"The feeling is mutual," she said softly, and I saw the desire shining back at me.

"We should probably stop, though. It's a little cold to keep going." I positioned the material of her bra back in place and let her shirt drop down before I pulled her to me and held her for a few moments.

She sighed softly. "I know you are right, but what a place to have sex, huh?"

I chuckled. "Yeah, that's for sure." I pulled back. "Something to remember when you come back to visit me in the summer."

"If you keep mentioning it, I just might have to do that."

"I'd like you to." I didn't know when or how it happened, but I'd become enamored with this woman. I knew she was leaving in less than a week, yet all I could picture was what the future might hold for us.

"Then maybe we can plan something," she replied.

"I think that's a good idea," I told her. "Let's get things packed up, and we can head out. I know we didn't eat the food I brought, but I know a great place not far from here where we can get fresh pastries."

"That sounds perfect," she replied.

We packed up our things and slowly made our way back up to the top.

"Wow, where did all the people come from?" she asked as we climbed back over the railing. About three dozen people were milling around the area, snapping pictures.

"I told you this is the best place to watch the sunrise."

She took my hand, pressing her body against my arm. "No, we had the best place to watch the sunrise."

I quickly kissed her lips before we hustled to the SUV. After we were inside, we drove north toward King's Beach, and I pulled down a side street to a little café that mostly locals frequented. The two of us enjoyed more coffee and ate breakfast at a small table in the corner as we discussed growing up with large families.

"That's pretty cool that you guys still have dinner together on Sundays. Our family only gets together on holidays because we are so spread out."

"It is nice, although there are times when I would prefer to avoid it."

"Why would you want to do that?"

She studied me as if she wasn't sure she should tell me, and I reached over the table and took her hand. "You can tell me anything, Coral, and I won't say anything to anyone."

"I appreciate that," she replied, then glanced out the window. "Do you think we could take a walk on the beach?"

"Sure, whatever you'd like to do."

We finished and then drove down to the beach area, where there wasn't as much snow. I found a parking spot along the street, and we walked hand in hand toward the water. Coral was quiet as she stared out over the lake and began to speak softly.

"I used to love Sunday dinner, but after my mother died, things began to change. Ethan and Riley were together then, and shortly after that, Cara and Bryan went through their drama."

"I haven't met them, right?"

She shook her head. "No, Cara is nine months pregnant. They live in Texas, but that's an entirely different story."

"Okay, you can tell me that one later."

"Anyway, after they got together and she moved, Candy and

Mike got involved with each other, and then Tim moved back to town, and Carmen and Tim quickly got back into a relationship."

"Back? What do you mean?"

"Tim and Carmen were high school sweethearts. He moved back to town because he works for Alaina, and the two of them were like magnets when he arrived in Millerstown."

"I knew his wife, Emily. Carmen reminds me of her."

"Yes, we know they look a lot alike."

I nodded. "So now that everyone has a mate, you're feeling left out?"

She shrugged and began to walk again. "I guess I started feeling that way before that. After Mom died, I lost my way. Mom and I were close, she was my best friend, and we talked about everything. I never felt that close to any of my siblings or my father. I didn't know who to turn to when she was gone, so I focused on my café, and my siblings just went on with life.

"It's like I'm an afterthought with most of them. They never share things with me, and I find out about things days, sometimes weeks, later than anyone else. No one reaches out to me about anything. When Carmen and Tim went through their pre-relationship drama, there was this huge text group, and I wasn't even part of it. No one even noticed, and that group had our friends in it too."

"What? You're kidding?"

She shook her head. "No, there is another family with six kids we grew up with. It's Riley's family. Sometimes, it was like we had eleven siblings because we were all close and spent vacations and holidays together."

"I can't even imagine that. Seven siblings were enough for me." I chuckled. "I guess getting lost in that many people would be easy."

"Yeah, and all of them are married too, so you have those

people and my people, and that's a lot of voices in a chat, but I wasn't one of them."

"I can see how that might have upset you."

"It did, but then I just forgot about it. They seem to do that with me, so it seemed only right to forget about them—most of the time."

I stopped her. "That sounds very lonely, Coral."

She blinked rapidly momentarily as if she were fighting back tears. "It is, Landan. I'm tired of always feeling like I'm on the outside of my family. Sometimes, I wish I had never moved back to town."

I pulled her into me and held her tightly. "I'm sorry that you feel that way and that they have made you feel it. That's wrong on so many levels."

She pulled back and stared at me. "Please don't say anything."

"I won't. It's not my place to say anything." At least right now, I thought to myself.

I held her for a few moments, and then we turned to look out over the water. She sighed softly. "I love this place, it's amazing."

"Yes, it is."

"It just makes me feel so much better. It's like I can feel myself coming back to life."

"I know what you mean." I glanced back. "Come here. I want to show you something."

We walked away from the beach and down a sidewalk for a while, and then we came to some monuments that talked about the lake and its depth. "Did you know that Mark Twain once came here and called it a healing place?"

"No, I had no idea."

I brushed some snow off one of the displays and pointed to a quote written there. "Read that. It's by Mark Twain."

Her voice lifted as she began to read. "*The air up there in the* clouds is very pure and fine. Bracing and delicious. And why shouldn't it be? It is the same the angels breathe."

"So yesterday, when you were at the top of the mountain in Heavenly, you were breathing the air of the angels."

She smiled and lifted sparkling blue eyes to me. "It's perfect, Landan. That's why I feel so at peace here. I am as close to heaven as possible and can feel my mom here with me."

"Yes, you can."

We looked over a few other monuments there and talked more about Mark Twain, then returned to the SUV. "Now where to?"

"I want to take you up to the Nevada side of the lake so you can see the water from there."

"Is it different?"

"It does look a little different," I stated.

"Then lead on," she said excitedly.

We worked our way north and pulled over occasionally when it was safe for her to take pictures. At one time she said, "I want to take as many of these as I can, so I can remind myself that it exists."

"Or you could just come back and visit."

"You keep saying that." She laughed. "You might not want me to come back."

Oh, I most definitely did want her to come back. There was no doubt about it. I had only known this woman for a day, and I was so bewitched by her that I didn't think I could ever not want the woman.

"I think you will be safe."

I drove up to eight thousand feet and gave her a great view of the lake and all the snow-capped mountains. The wind was blustery, but she didn't seem to mind.

Then we headed back toward the lake and continued our trip around the north shore. I took her to Sand Harbor State Park, where I knew the lots would be plowed. They also took great care in keeping the walking paths around the lake cleared, and when she saw the beauty of the blue and green water around the rocks, she gasped.

"It looks like a picture, Landan. This is incredible."

I grinned. "It rivals you." The words were out without thinking.

She threw her head back and laughed. "Give me a break. No, really, it is absolutely stunning."

I pulled her back against me, lacing my hands over her stomach. "And so are you, Coral."

She glanced back at me. "You're just saying that."

I shook my head. "No, I'm not. I don't say things I don't mean."

She turned in my arms, wrapping her arms around my neck. "Well, I thank you."

I kissed her slowly, and then another couple began to approach us, and we pulled apart and started to walk again. The wind was biting here, but Coral didn't seem to mind.

We found an area near a group of rocks that blocked the wind and stood there for a long time. I loved that she saw the beauty the way I did. Neither of us had to speak. We were both comfortable with the silence of nature around us.

Finally, she shivered, and I tucked her closer to me. "How about we head to the gift shop, and then we can go someplace warmer and get something to eat."

"I like that idea. All this fresh air makes me hungry."

I hoped she wasn't disappointed with my choice of location. I had a feeling once she saw it, she wouldn't be.

CHAPTER ELEVEN

CORAL

I could not have asked for a better day. After walking along the lake, my fingers and cheeks felt like ice cubes, but it had been worth it. We visited the gift shop, and I bought some trinkets for my employees.

Landan and I climbed back into his vehicle and got back on the road. I had no idea where we were going, and I didn't care. All I knew was I was in this incredible place with a fantastic man. I would have gone anywhere and done anything to continue my day.

As we drove, my phone rang, and it was Monica's ringtone. I had my phone on silent, but Monica's number would always ring, no matter what.

"Hello?" I said as I picked up the phone, instantly feeling anxious that something might be wrong at home.

"Oh my god! You are still alive! I thought you might have fallen off a cliff somewhere."

I laughed. "No, I haven't fallen off a cliff."

"Whew, I was worried about you because I hadn't heard from you."

"I'm fine. How are things back there?"

"Everything is good here. There are no problems."

"I thought for sure that you were calling with a problem."

"Not at all. I was just worried when I didn't hear from you. How is it out there? Are you having fun?"

"I can't believe I will say this, but I am so glad they made me come. It is incredible, Monica—absolutely stunning. I can't get over the beauty of the area."

"Are you getting a chance to sightsee?"

"I am, and I have a private guide."

"What?"

"One of the neighbors, Landan, is taking me around the lake."

"Landan, oh, la, la! Is he cute?"

I peered toward Landan. "Yes, very."

"Oh my god! I can't wait to hear everything about him! Send me some more pictures! I have to live vicariously through you."

"I will when we hang up."

"Okay, I won't keep you. I am so glad that you are having a great time. You deserve it. Just don't fall in love with the place and not come back."

"Damn, you caught me. That's exactly what I was thinking."

"Oh, no! You have to come back."

"Yeah, sadly, I will, but I am already thinking about when I can return," I told her. "I might have to come back in the summer to experience the lake and not the skiing."

Landan grinned and then winked when he turned my way.

"I wish I could go with you. I would love to see it. A friend of mine visited there and said it was the best place he had ever been."

"I have to agree with your friend."

"Alright, you go have fun. I'll email you the numbers for today when I finish them."

"Sounds good. I'll talk to you later, Monica."

After we said goodbye, I checked my phone to see I had

twenty-seven texts and six phone calls. "Whoops! Looks like everyone has been searching for me."

I had purposefully turned it on silent so my family wouldn't bother me.

His head snapped my way. "You didn't tell them you were coming with me?"

"I might not have mentioned it," I replied as I began to type into the group text message that I was okay and having a great time with Landan and would see them later. No sooner had I sent it when Carmen called, but I ignored it and put my phone away.

Landan laughed. "Did you send them a message?"

"I did, and I told them I was with you."

"Maybe you should call them and let them hear your voice."

"I am almost thirty-seven years old. I think I can take care of myself."

"Almost thirty-seven, huh?"

"Yeah, you are about to have a birthday. How old will you be?"

"I'm turning forty."

And damn, did he look good for his age. I held that part back. "Have you ever been married?"

"I almost got married last year."

"What happened? I mean, if you don't mind me asking."

He shook his head. "No, I don't mind you asking, but let's table this discussion for a little while because we are here."

As he spoke, he turned off the roadway and down a narrow street where a tall black gate blocked our path. "Where are we? Don't tell me we are going to hop the fence and break the law again."

"You'll find out in a minute." He chuckled as he pushed a button on the visor and a gate began to open in front of us.

"Wait, how can you get in the gate?"

"Because this is my place."

"Oh, that's right, you own property around here. Do you rent this place out?" We drove through the gate, and I ogled the beautiful home. It was dark brown with black accents.

"No, this place is for me alone."

"Don't you live at the other house?" I asked as he parked.

"No, I only stay there when the family is in town. The rest of the time, I am here."

"Wow, it's amazing."

"Wait till you see the view."

We climbed out, and he told me to grab my bags before he led me to the front door. The minute I stepped in, I fell in love with the place. It was all done in earth tones, and unlike the house we were staying in that looked like a showroom, this one looked loved and lived in.

I was immediately drawn to the glass wall on the other side. "Holy shit," I murmured. "This is amazing, Landan."

"I thought you might like it," he said as he came to stand behind me and put his hands on my shoulders.

"I can't believe you live here. What I wouldn't give for a view like this every day."

He stepped around me and reached for the latch on the door. "In the summer, I can open all of these."

"What an incredible open space you would have." I stepped through the door behind him and moved to the railing. Below was a stone path leading to a small beach with a long wooden walkway out into the water where a boat could be moored. Around the beach area were large rocks you could sit on to enjoy the view. I was in awe and kept telling myself to close my mouth, but I couldn't.

"You like it?"

"Like it? You probably shouldn't have shown me this. I might never leave."

He chuckled. "You asked about why I didn't get married. Believe it or not, I bought this house for Eve and me to live in. She thought it was too far from the fun of South Lake Tahoe."

"Wait, she didn't appreciate the view?"

"I'm sure she liked it, but not once did I ever see the look on her face that you have now."

"What type of look is that?"

"A look of wonder. That's how I feel whenever I step out here. It's like it's hard to believe that this much beauty is available for me to see every day."

"Is that why you two didn't get married? Because she didn't like this place?" That was hard to believe.

His face shuttered slightly as he looked away. "No, I wish it was that simple. On the night of our rehearsal dinner, I found her having sex with my best friend."

"What?" I practically shrieked. First of all, that was wrong on so many levels. Second, how could any woman walk away from the man before me?

"Yeah, it was a rough night."

I put my hand on his arm. "Landan, I'm so sorry that happened to you."

"I got over it."

"She didn't deserve you."

"I agree."

"Has there ever been anyone else?"

"Not really. I have dated quite a few women, but nothing as serious. There were other issues with Eve, too, but that one took the cake."

"What other issues?"

He turned sideways to study me. "She didn't want kids."

I winced, knowing that he put a kibosh on whatever future we might have had. Not that I was thinking about futures—okay, that's a lie.

"I assume you want them."

"I do. What about you?"

I gnawed on my bottom lip for a moment and then sighed. "Not that it matters, but I can't have kids."

I saw his frown when I glanced his way. "Can't have them?"

I shook my head. "No, I was in a horseback riding accident when I was seventeen and landed on a stick that went through my lower abdomen. It ruined my uterus, and I had a partial hysterectomy."

"Holy crap, Coral. I'm so sorry."

I shrugged. "I got used to the idea of never having kids a long time ago. As I got older, I figured I would probably marry someone who already had some, or maybe I would adopt one."

"Would you be open to adopting?"

"Yeah, probably."

"My four younger siblings are all adopted."

I cocked my head, trying to picture the ones I had seen. "I didn't know that."

"Laney, Lily, Lucas, and Levi were all adopted as babies. My mom had an emergency hysterectomy after Leo was born."

"Wow, I had no idea. They look so much like you guys with the dark hair that I would never have thought they weren't blood-related."

"Most people don't know, and we don't say anything. They are as much family as the rest of us are."

"So you'd be open to adopting?"

He nodded. "I would. I had even approached Eve with that, but she said she enjoyed traveling and going out too much to be strapped down with a kid."

I rolled my eyes. "Strapped down. Well, sorry, but I think you are better off without her."

"I think I am too, now, at least. It took me a while to lick my wounds."

"You still friends with that guy?"

He laughed and turned back to the railing. "Haven't spoken to him since that night."

"Good for you."

I shifted and looked around his deck. "You have a hot tub." I grinned. "Is that why you told me to bring my bathing suit? Was this your idea all along? Get me back to your place alone?"

He smirked as he turned my way and pulled me by my jacket to get closer. "It might have been, but I wouldn't have brought you here if I thought you weren't having a good time."

I put my arms on his shoulders. "Every moment I have been with you has been a great time, Landan."

He brushed his hand over my hair, then cupped my cheek. "I have to agree with you, Coral. I've loved every moment with you."

I leaned forward and kissed him slowly. "Then how about you show me the rest of your house, and we put our bathing suits on and get in that hot tub to have more fun."

"You keep talking like that, and we might not make it in the water."

"Oh, no." I stepped back and eyed the gigantic hot tub. "We are getting in. What happens once we do is another thing."

He bent over and picked me up, tossing me over his shoulder as he turned toward the hot tub. "Who needs bathing suits then!"

I laughed and slapped his back. "Put me down! We are going to start this adventure off decent."

"Fine," Landan said, pretending to be disappointed, but I saw in his eyes when my feet were on the ground that he was anything but. "Come on, I'll show you where you can change."

Landan gave me a quick tour of the house, and the beauty spellbound me. No matter where you were, you had an incredible view of the lake. What I wouldn't give for a view like this.

"Do you want to change in the guest room or use my room?" He paused in the hallway between the two rooms. I eyed him carefully, seeing the hope in his eyes.

"You know I will end up in your room anyway, so I might as well change there."

He groaned in a good way as his head rolled back on his shoulders. "You're killing me, Coral."

I giggled as he pulled me into his room, and then he let go of me immediately and stepped away as if he didn't trust himself. I forced myself not to laugh, loving the power I had over him. It had been so long since I had felt this sexual chemistry with anyone.

"The bathroom is in there. You can make yourself comfortable. There is a robe behind the door if you want to use that. I will get the hot tub ready."

He quickly slipped past me and closed the door behind him. I glanced around his room, loving the colors and décor he had. Then I walked to the window and stared out with a happy sigh. I really could get used to this. It was a shame that my life was on the other side of the country.

However, I was here now, and I would enjoy every moment of it.

CHAPTER TWELVE

LANDAN

That woman was going to drive me wild. It had started when we were making out on the rock at Emerald's Bay, and even though we hadn't kissed much since, the chemistry had been bubbling under the surface with every touch and kiss we had shared.

I wasn't sure how you could feel this much for someone after only knowing them briefly, but it was as if she were made for me. She was perfect. She was active, sassy, and had a great sense of humor. She could be cute and then look at me like a sensual goddess and melt the bones in my body.

I went out and removed the cover from the hot tub, then turned on soft music and went to get a few snacks ready, along with a bottle of wine. We hadn't eaten the fruit earlier, so I put that on the tray, along with some crackers and cheese I had for the off chance of having guests.

That didn't happen often, but occasionally a friend popped over. Never a female friend. In the year I had lived here, I had never had a woman over here alone. Some had come to parties but never stayed. Eve was the only woman who was ever here alone when I had first shown her the house.

I thought about the difference between Eve and Coral. They weren't even in the same category. Eve was superficial and rude, and Coral was loving and adventurous. I didn't think there was a superficial cell in her body. She was the kind of woman whom I could have only hoped to meet, and here she was, in my house and about to climb into my hot tub with me—and hopefully my bed.

Coral looked cute with my fluffy blue robe wrapped around her. "You know, this might have to go home with me."

Can I come too? I wanted to ask but knew I didn't want to be anywhere but here. What would she say if I told her I wanted her to stay?

"Perfect. I just got some snacks for us. Let me change, and I'll be right back."

As I returned to the bedroom, I found her clothes thrown haphazardly on the side chair. I grinned.

I removed the bathing suit from my drawer and continued thinking about her staying here. I shook my head at myself. We barely knew one another. Why would she want to come here to be with me?

Jesus, I needed to get my head on straight. Although not as nice, I had a second robe in my closet and wrapped myself up before returning to the living room. She stood in front of the glass wall, a glass of wine in her hand and a cracker in the other.

"Couldn't wait for me, could you?"

She giggled. "I'm starving! I can't help myself."

She helped me carry everything outside and then shivered as she removed the robe. There was no way I would miss watching her climb into the tub, and I got a partial hard-on as I checked out the curves of her body. She glanced back and laughed. "Enjoying the view?"

"More than you know," I replied, then tossed my robe over hers after setting the tray beside the hot tub.

She wasn't shy to watch me, and I moaned as I slipped under the water. "Enjoying the view?" I taunted back at her.

"More than you know," she said with a smirk and turned toward the lake. "I mean, the lake is incredible. How could I not enjoy it."

I laughed. "Yeah, right. That's not what we were talking about."

She grinned, and I sat beside her and let myself enjoy the moment.

"This is perfect," she commented a few minutes later.

"What, the hot tub?"

"The hot tub, the scenery, the wine. And the company... it's not that bad either."

I looked at her. She was watching me, a playful look in her eye. "You're right. The company isn't half-bad. In fact, it's pretty much one hundred percent perfect."

"Now, I wouldn't say that." She laughed loudly.

We continued to stare at one another for a few seconds, and then she set her wineglass behind her and moved toward me. I didn't do anything but watch her. I was going to let her lead where she wanted this to go.

When she got closer to me, she took the glass from my hands and set it behind me, then she turned and sat with her back against my chest and her head on my shoulder.

I pulled her tightly to me and knew there was no doubt she could feel the erection I was sporting. Neither of us said a word for a long time, and eventually, I kissed down her neck. I heard her breath hitch, and she put her hand over mine and moved it to cover her breast.

She turned her face toward me, and I captured her lips in a hungry kiss as my other hand shifted lower on her stomach toward the edge of her bikini. She didn't stop me, so I continued. At first, I ran my hand over her bathing suit, but the need to touch her intimately was too strong, so I retraced my steps and slipped under the thin material.

She whimpered into my mouth at the first touch, and I deepened the kiss as I ran my fingers through her folds and found that bundle of nerves that was so important.

The water was hot around us, but she made me burn. I continued to touch her, adding pressure and moving quicker, and she whimpered into my mouth again. I felt her body climbing and was amazed at her responsiveness to my touch. I had never had a woman get so turned on by just my fingers, which made my balls ache.

She pulled away from the kiss, laying her hand back on my shoulder as her breath came in pants. "Oh my god!" she murmured, "Yes!"

Hearing those words made my dick throb, but I wasn't going to stop until I made her come. It took only another minute before her body tensed and twitched, and she slapped a hand over her mouth to stifle the cry of pleasure. I wanted to hear her shout, but I wouldn't push her.

However, I peeled her hand back and retook her mouth as I lightened the pressure and let her work through the last of her orgasm. Eventually, I shifted back and looked down at her. Her cheeks were flushed, and her eyes were glassy. "You are beautiful," I murmured toward her.

"You made me feel beautiful," she replied.

I kissed her again as I removed my hand, and then I sat back, trying not to think about the fact that my dick was throbbing so hard, but she wasn't ready for things to end. The moment I sat back in the seat, she moved before me and wiggled a bit. Then she lifted her bikini bottoms and tossed them over the side. I watched them land as my dick kicked hard against the confines of my suit.

She reached behind her and untied her top, sending it sailing over the side, too. "I think someone has too many clothes on," she said seductively.

Coral didn't need to say that twice. I was already working on the tie of my suit, and a few seconds later, it landed beside her bottoms. "Now what are you going to do?" I asked her as she was a few feet away from me.

She glanced around as if she were checking for something, and then she stood up, and my gaze devoured her heavy breasts. I stroked my cock, dying to have her touch me but wanting to know what she would do first. She popped up on the tub's edge, reaching for the robe. She pulled it around her shoulders and sat back, spreading her legs. I about lost my mind as I got a peek at her most intimate parts.

She didn't need to say a word as I practically dove between her thighs. I licked at her sensitive flesh, slowly easing a finger into her as she grabbed my head and leaned farther back. I reached up with my other hand and palmed her breast, kneading it rougher than I intended, but she was driving me wild. The taste of her flesh was like the best wine money could buy, and I lost myself in the taste of her on my tongue as I pushed in a second finger.

She was already climbing, and I knew she wouldn't take long to hit that pinnacle again. She pushed her hips forward, holding my head with one hand as she began to whimper softly. "Please, please, oh, God, please!"

I moved quickly, rotating my tongue faster as my fingers stroked in and out more rapidly. I felt it just before she exploded around my fingers. Her body jerked as she came harder than the first time, and I lapped at her, tasting her thick juices and feeling like I would die if I didn't get in her soon.

I stood, shoving the robe from her shoulders in one motion, then picked her up and turned around to set her on my lap. Within a few seconds, I was seated deep within her, and she curled herself around me, nipping and kissing my neck. She rotated her hips in small circles and pulled back until I was almost out before she pushed forward and took me in again.

"Fuck," I growled against her neck and worked my lips back to her mouth. "You feel so fucking good, Coral."

She didn't reply in words. She took my mouth again and continued rolling her hips. Like her, I wouldn't last long, but before I hit that point of no return, she ground herself against me hard. I felt her body climbing again, and I held back as much as possible until I knew she was getting close again. The thought of her coming around my cock threw me over the edge, and a second after I came, she was right there with me, squeezing me with every pulse.

We calmed down but didn't break apart. I held Coral there, never wanting to let her go. I wasn't sure how it had happened, but this woman had broken through the shell around my heart and somehow wormed her way inside in only a day.

Finally, after a few minutes, she shifted back. "I'm not sure I could walk right now if I had to."

I laughed huskily. "No, probably not after that. It's a good thing we are in the hot tub."

She wiggled off my lap and sat across from me. "I have to admit, that was almost as incredible as the view."

"Almost?" I asked as I reached for her wineglass and handed it to her before collecting mine.

"Okay, maybe it was even better than the view." She held up her glass. "Might I propose a toast?"

"Of course." I held my glass up and waited.

"To whatever might be, and enjoying the moments accompanying it."

I grinned. "I like that. To whatever might be, and the moments that go with it."

Our glasses touched, and as we stared at one another and sipped our wine, I hoped those moments never ended.

CHAPTER THIRTEEN

CORAL

Perhaps I should have been embarrassed by my behavior, but I wasn't. It had been a long time since I had been with someone, and I was old enough to do what I wanted when I wanted and with whom I wanted. Landan didn't seem to be disappointed.

We remained quiet, basking in the glow of sex as we snacked on the food he had brought out.

"There are a lot of clouds over there," I commented as I took in the distant sky.

"That is South Lake Tahoe. You can see a storm coming in." He frowned. "It's earlier than expected. It wasn't supposed to be here until tonight."

"Should we get going?"

He turned to me. "Do you want to go?"

I quickly shook my head. "No, if I had my choice, I'd stay here for the rest of my vacation."

He gave me a lopsided grin. "Then stay."

I laughed. "What? I was joking—kinda."

"I'm not. If you'd rather stay here, we can. I'm good with that. We could run down to the market; it's only a couple blocks away. We could get some more food, and then come back and stay here."

"What about our families?"

"What about them? Isn't this your vacation?"

"Yes, but don't you want to be with your family?"

He grabbed my ankle and pulled me to sit on his lap. "And miss out on spending as much time with a beautiful woman as I can? Hell no! Besides, I see them enough."

He was right. This was my vacation, and I saw my family all the time. "I don't have any clothes with me."

He shrugged. "Do you need them? I mean, I'm happy to have you in my robe."

I laughed. "Oh, you only want me here for the sex. Is that it?"

"I'd be lying if I said that it wasn't on my mind to have my way with you at least a dozen more times, but I enjoy your company too."

He won me over, and I wrapped my arms around his neck. "Then let's stay here. We can stay in our robes and make love anytime we want, as much as we want."

"I like the way you think." He kissed me and then looked over my shoulder. "But we should probably change and go to the store. Then we should let our families know we are safe and staying put."

"If I have to," I whined, but I wasn't upset. He was right. The least I could do was tell them I was okay and wouldn't be home tonight.

We wrapped ourselves up and then quickly went inside. I made Landan wait for me to get dressed alone because I had a feeling if we had done it together, we wouldn't have gotten out anytime soon. By the look out the window, the storm was moving fast.

We left shortly after that and went to the market. It was a quaint place that Landan said the locals favored. We collected quite a bit, and I wondered how long he thought I'd stay. I didn't say anything, though.

The clouds loomed over us as we stepped out, and the snow was already falling when we pulled through his gate. This time, he put the Expedition in the garage.

Once everything was unpacked, we made sandwiches, and I dug my phone out as we sat at the table. I had a dozen more texts and two more phone calls. One was from my father. I knew he had to be worried if he called me.

I sat back in my seat. "I need to call them and let them know I am okay."

"Do you want privacy?"

"No." I hit dial on my father's number and was surprised when Silvia answered.

"We were getting worried about you. The storm came sooner than expected. When will you get back?"

"I'm fine, and I'm not coming back tonight."

"What? Where are you?"

"I am with Landan at his house in North Lake Tahoe. We came up here before the storm and decided to stay here."

"For how long?"

"I don't know, at least overnight."

She grew quiet and chuckled. "Well, I guess your vacation is going better than you expected."

I grinned. "I guess it is."

"I hope you two have a wonderful time. I will let everyone know you are safe."

"Thanks, Silvia. I appreciate that and tell them to leave me alone. I have two dozen messages. They need to all relax and stop."

"I will. Enjoy yourself, Coral. You deserve some fun."

"Thanks, Silvia. I'll talk to you later."

After I hung up, Landan grinned. "Were they upset?"

"No, I think Silvia is happy I am enjoying myself. I don't care what the others think."

"I should call my mom."

I grinned at him. "Do you want privacy?"

He laughed. "No, I'm going to put it on speaker."

"Oh, wow! Speaker! Well, la-de-da!"

Landan called his mother's phone and set it down as the ringing filled the room.

"Hey, Landan. I was wondering when I would hear from you. Tim was over here a little while ago wondering where you were."

"He was probably more wondering where his sister-in-law was. Coral and I are up at my place. We're going to stay the night. The storm came in faster than expected."

"Do you have anything to eat?"

"We just ran to the market right before the snow began."

"Okay, good. Well, you two enjoy it there. Tell Coral hello, and I am sure she is enjoying the view from your place."

I waved. "She says hello. I have you on speaker."

"Oh, hello, Coral. Are you enjoying his place?"

"It's beautiful here. The house and the view." I wanted to add, 'and the company,' but I kept that to myself.

"He does have a great place. Well, you two have fun, and let me know when you are coming back." She paused. "Have you heard from Luna? I'm not sure where she is right now."

"No, I haven't. Do you want me to try reaching out to her?"

"No, that's alright. I left her a message. She is probably with Marcus, and I know she forgets everything else when she is with him."

"That sounds like Luna. Let me know if you need me to do something."

"I will, Landan."

"Bye, Mom."

He hit the button. "And now we are safely away from our families. What will we do while we are stuck in this house?"

I glanced around. "I guess we could watch a movie."

"Do you want to watch a movie?"

"Sure." I popped a chip into my mouth. "Or we could have sex again and then watch a movie."

"We could put a movie on and have sex while we watch the snowfall."

I laughed. "Yes, that's perfect, as long as we aren't watching some horror movie."

"No horror and an action movie would probably ruin the moment, too."

"True." I nodded.

"How about we finish watching *City of Angels*?"

"Aw, you are such a romantic."

"I am, but don't tell anyone. It's a closely kept secret."

"Your secret is safe with me," I told him.

We finished eating, and then he disappeared into the bedroom. When he came out, he was wearing lounge pants and a T-shirt. "I put a pair of pajama bottoms and a T-shirt on the bed for you. Might be more comfortable to lie on the couch in those."

"See, romantic." I pretended to swoon, and he shook his head at me.

"Go change, and I'll find the movie."

The pants were big on me, of course, but they had a draw-string so I could tie them up. I left the hem long to cover my feet and removed my sweater and bra, pulling on the soft light-blue T-shirt. I loved that I was wearing Landan's clothes. It made me feel even closer to him.

He had the movie ready, and we curled up on the couch together under a blanket. I was leaning against his chest, and he had his arm wrapped around my waist as the movie started.

We weren't ten minutes in when his hand began to move

slowly, running over my belly in circles. His fingers brushed the underside of my breast, and I shivered. He shifted his hand under the T-shirt and continued, this time more purposefully, as he cupped one breast and rubbed his thumb over the nipple before moving to the other.

My hand was tightly on his, and I squeezed it as shivers of delight coursed down my spine into the apex of my thighs.

He kissed the side of my head, moving down until he reached my ear. His breath was hot against my ear, bringing goosebumps over my flesh. His chuckle was deep as he nibbled on my ear, and my eyes closed to enjoy the sensation.

His hand slipped down my stomach, and he slowly untied the drawstring. Once it was undone, he shifted his hand under and moaned when he found I wasn't wearing any panties.

I spread my legs a little wider so he could reach better, and he quickly began building the tension inside me. I was amazed he could do that so easily with only his hand.

I tried to move, but he held me still. "No, I want to feel you shatter against me again."

"Ah," I gasped as he pressed harder. His words took me up a notch, and I didn't take long to spill over.

I was barely done when he shifted from behind me and sat on his knees at the other end of the couch. He yanked at my pants, and I raised my hips so he could pull them down. Before I could do anything else, he was pushing me back to put his face between my thighs again. I wasn't going to tell him no, even though I was dying to taste him.

I was almost to the top again when he pulled back and stood. He yanked off his shirt, tossed it aside, then pushed his pants down, and I got the first good look at him. I wanted to weep at how beautiful he was. I reached out and wrapped my hand around the length of his shaft, and he moaned as his head fell forward, his eyes barely open as he watched me.

I sat up, shifted in front of him, and slowly licked the end of his cock as I stared up at him. He inhaled sharply as I wrapped my mouth around him and licked the underside with my tongue.

His hand landed on the back of my head as I began to move over him, and he only let me do it for a moment before he jerked back. "I can't handle that mouth on me right now."

He moved to the end of the couch and pulled my ankles so I was lying flat. Then he started to lay his body over mine, and I quickly removed the T-shirt I wore and dropped it beside the couch.

His body felt incredible over mine, and I ran my foot up the back of his calf as he kissed me until I was dizzy. We made love slowly this time, and he stared me in the eye when he entered me. I swear I saw things in his eyes that shouldn't have been there, but I felt the same way.

I pulled his mouth to mine so neither of us would say something we regretted. We fit so perfectly together. I loved every inch of him I could touch, and he ran his hands and mouth over my entire body. When we came together again a while later, we stared at one another as we crashed over the top.

I'd never felt so connected to another human being. It was the most beautiful thing I had ever experienced. After cleaning up, we curled on the couch naked, and we drifted off to sleep as Meg Ryan and Nicholas Cage played another romantic scene on the television.

14

CHAPTER FOURTEEN

LANDAN

I had been with many women, but I could not recall one woman I had felt as complete with as I did when I was with Coral. Making love to her was more than sex—a lot more. The problem was, I didn't know what it meant for me or, more importantly, for us.

I was thinking about that as I felt her relax into sleep in my arms. Part of me felt like this was exactly as it was supposed to be, but another part of me—the intelligent part—said there was no way I could feel this for someone in a day.

I woke with a start, and my eyes flashed open to find Luna and Marcus standing in the middle of the living room, covered in snow. Coral was obviously awake, too, as she'd pulled the covers up to her chin.

"Sorry, I didn't realize we'd be walking in on you guys that way." She laughed cheekily. "Do you want us to go back outside so you can get dressed?" She bent down and picked up my pants, tossing them over us.

"That might be nice, or at least go in the other room."

"How about we go out and come through the garage to take our coats and boots off?"

103

"Better idea," I grumbled at her, and the two of them scuddled out the door, but not before I saw Marcus checking Coral out and asking, "Who is that?"

Coral laughed abruptly. "I wasn't expecting that."

"Me either. Come on. Let's grab our clothes while we can and get dressed in my room."

She bounced up and tried to keep the blanket around her as she collected our stuff. I wasn't as modest and walked naked through my living room, following her into the bedroom.

"Does she routinely do that?"

"Do what? Walk in on me while I'm with a woman?"

She cocked her head. "Well, that too, but I meant walk into your house."

"She has a key. She's the only one with one, and no to your other question, by the way."

"Good to know." She used the restroom and came out dressed in pajama pants but no top. I made sure to enjoy the moment.

"You planning on walking around like that? I won't be the only one to enjoy it if you do."

"Funny!" She rolled her eyes. "I'm going to put my bra on. It's one thing to be free when it's just us, but I don't know Marcus."

"You don't really know me either," I said and immediately regretted it when her brow furrowed.

She pulled her top over her head, and I went to stand beside her. "I'm sorry. That didn't come out right."

"No, you're right," she replied. "Is it weird that I feel like I have known you a lot longer than a couple of days?"

"It's really only been one and a half."

"True. Is it weird? Maybe you don't think so, but this kind of stuff doesn't happen where I come from."

"What kind of stuff?"

She shrugged. "I don't know, magic." She winced. "That

probably sounds stupid to you. I'm sure you don't even feel the same."

I held her face. "I think magic is the perfect word. I was thinking earlier about how incredible you are and how well suited we are. Not just with sex, but everything."

Her face relaxed. "You feel it too?"

I nodded. "I do, but what bothers me is what it means."

"What do you mean?"

"I really like you, Coral, but you're leaving in a few days. My life is here, and yours is back east. I don't even know what state you live in."

She cradled my face. "I live in a little place called Miller-stown in the big state of Pennsylvania."

"Okay, so you live in Pennsylvania. I don't know what that means for us."

She sighed. "I think that means that we enjoy every moment we have together, and if it's meant to be, then maybe I can come see you again next summer."

"Next summer?" I pursed my lips. "Why do I already feel like that is too far off?"

"Landan, you are right. We live on opposite coasts, but I don't want to look a gift horse in the mouth. Let's enjoy what we have and not put any labels on it."

"You're right. I'm sorry."

"Don't be sorry. I'm glad to know I'm not the only one feeling this."

"You're not," I told her and brushed her hair back, then leaned forward and kissed her just as there was a knock on the door.

"Are you decent now?" Luna called.

"We will be out in a minute," I yelled back at her, then said to Coral, "Sorry about the interruption. Looks like we are going to have company tonight."

"That's okay, I don't mind. I think your sister is nice."

I laughed. "You don't know her yet." I took her hand and led her back to the living room. My sister and Marcus were in the kitchen digging through the fridge.

"I am so glad you thought to go shopping."

"Why are you here?" I asked as I retrieved the bottle of wine Coral and I had been drinking.

"We got stuck in the storm, and there was no way we would make it back home in his car."

"You aren't driving your truck?"

He shook his head. "No, man. I thought we'd be back before the storm came."

"Where were you guys?"

"Over in Reno. We should have left earlier. Why are you guys here? Were you skiing up here?"

"No, I took Coral sightseeing, and we stopped here to use the hot tub."

She turned to look out the window. "Oh, it's working?"

"Of course, it's working."

"The last time I was here, it was out of commission," she stated and pulled out the chicken breasts that I had bought. "You have plans for these?"

"Why?"

"Well, since we crashed your date, I could at least cook dinner."

I waved my hand toward the kitchen. "By all means."

Luna finally addressed Coral. "I'm sorry to intrude."

"That's quite all right."

"Marcus, this is Coral. Coral, this is my sister's sometimes boyfriend, Marcus."

"I'm more like her boy toy," Marcus said with a grin.

Coral laughed. "It's nice to meet you."

"You too, and sorry for interrupting."

"It will be fun to have company." She grinned my way.

She was right, and the four of us laughed and shared

stories throughout dinner. After dinner, we put the awning over the hot tub and climbed in. Since Luna stayed here occasionally, she kept a bathing suit in the guest room. Even though he said he could go naked, I loaned Marcus a pair of swim trunks.

Luna hooted. "Yeah, like Coral wants to see your ass. Don't you see what she already has?"

It was much colder this time, and the wind was whipping around, but the awning helped keep most of the snow off of us while we continued to joke around.

"Coral, I have to tell you, your skin is gorgeous." My sister got in her face, causing Coral to back up against the tub wall.

"Um, thanks."

"What do you use on it?"

"You must be the sister who owns the skincare company?"

"Yeah, I am. How did you know?" She backed up and went to sit beside Marcus again.

"Landan told me about it."

She gave me an annoyed look. "I bet he told you about the nose hair conditioner that I made him use."

Coral started laughing. "Yes, he did."

I looked at Marcus, who was trying not to be seen by looking anywhere but at us. "Come on, Marcus, tell us the truth. You've used it. What did you think of it?"

"Um, sure, I loved it." His voice went up an octave, like he was trying to sound chipper.

"See, he loved it," Luna said, and behind her, Marcus was exaggeratedly shaking his head. Coral and I laughed, and Luna whipped her head back to him. "Are you lying to me?"

"Come on, baby, it's weird. That's all I'm saying. Some hair just shouldn't be conditioned. I get beards and all, but not nose hair."

"You're kidding! You told me you loved it and used it all the time! What have you been doing with the tubes I sent you?"

"Um, giving them as gifts," he said with wide eyes and grimaced as she dramatically sighed.

"You are a loser. All of you are losers."

"Can we change the subject before I am cockblocked for the rest of the night?" Marcus said quickly as he leaned toward Luna and tried to kiss her neck.

"You're already cockblocked, buddy. You can sleep on the couch." She said the words, but I saw the smile on her face. There was no way she would let him sleep on the couch.

The thing with them was that they liked each other, and when she was in town, they spent a lot of time together, but when she left, they went back to their lives without a problem. I glanced at Coral. I wasn't sure I could do that.

For the rest of the evening, we enjoyed ourselves. We laughed and even played a game of Scrabble when we got out of the hot tub. It wasn't until midnight that Coral and I turned in, and about ten minutes after we did, the headboard in the guest room started knocking on the wall.

Coral jerked up and stared at the wall, her mouth hanging open in mock horror. "Does she do that often?"

I was laughing at the expression on her face. "Once in a while, but I am usually asleep already."

She threw herself back on the pillow with a grunt and then covered her hand over her mouth as she laughed. The knocking got worse, and then she winked at me and started moaning loudly.

I rolled to my side, laughing into the pillow as she got louder and louder. "Oh, god! Yes! Yes! Keep going! Oh, god!" She started moaning again, and the knocking on the wall stopped, and laughter could be heard through the wall.

"Go, Landan!" Marcus yelled, and I pulled Coral to me and kissed her hard.

"You are incredible."

"You're mighty fine yourself," she replied.

108

"I'm glad we came here. I hope you didn't mind my sister too much."

"No, I love Luna, she's great. She reminds me of Riley." She grew quiet momentarily. "You know, I had more fun tonight with you and your sister than I've had with any of my siblings in as long as I can remember."

"I'm glad. Luna and I are really close."

"She's pretty cool."

"She thinks you are pretty cool, too."

"She said that?"

I nodded. "She did while we put the wineglasses in the kitchen. I think her exact words were that we were good together. She liked that I was smiling and laughing. I haven't done that a lot this last year."

Coral ran her fingers over my face. "I'm sorry things haven't been great."

"It's okay. I needed the time to focus on myself and my life so I would be ready for you when you showed up."

She stared back at me. "Do you mean that?"

I nodded. "I know it's odd, but I can't stop thinking about how perfect we are together. We just fit. I've been looking for that kind of relationship for most of my life."

"I have too," she replied.

"Then let's do everything we can to continue it."

She whispered her reply as she leaned forward. "It's a deal."

CHAPTER FIFTEEN

CORAL

I woke up to warm arms around me and a soft kiss on my temple as those arms pulled me tightly over to his side of the bed. I blinked at the bright light and finally opened them enough to see out the window.

I sat up, jumped out of bed, and ran to the window. "Holy crap, Landan! Look at all the snow that fell."

"I saw it when I opened the curtains." He sat up. "Come back to bed."

"Can we go skiing?"

"Now?"

I nodded excitedly, then ran back to the bed and jumped on it. "Please!"

He laughed. "Yes, but not yet. It's not even six yet."

I glanced at the clock beside the bed, noting it was five forty. I sighed. "Fine, I'll wait." I climbed back off the bed and went into the bathroom to use the toilet, and then I used my finger to brush my teeth the best I could.

I ran back to the bed and jumped on it, crashing into him, and he laughed again. "You're like a kid on Christmas morning."

I grinned saucily at him. "Are you my present?"

"Oh, you can unwrap me any day you want."

I began pulling the covers back from him and exposed his bare chest. I leaned forward and started to brush kisses over it, moving slowly lower. He shifted a bit, and I put my hand down over his groin to find he was already hard as a rock and ready to go. I grinned at him and began to tug at his waistband. He helped me get them off his hips, and then I took him in my hand and stroked him slowly as I stared into his eyes.

I loved the soft brown color of his irises. I loved everything about this man so much that my heart wanted to burst. I closed my eyes so he wouldn't see how I felt and bent over to take him into my mouth. Like the night before, he didn't let me go too long before pushing me away and removing the T-shirt I slept in.

We made love slowly, and we lay on our sides afterward, staring at one another. I never wanted to leave this man. I wanted to stay here with him forever.

A few minutes later, Landan rolled to his back and closed his eyes. "You okay?" I asked.

"Yeah, we should get dressed and get something to eat. We can hit Big Springs."

"Okay," I replied, noticing his demeanor had changed in a big way. He climbed out of bed and went to use the bathroom.

While he was gone, I pulled out the clothes I had brought if we went skiing. He returned to the bedroom. "Do you mind if I take a quick shower?"

"Go ahead," he stated, but didn't look my way. I gathered my things and went into the bathroom, peering back at him to see him pulling clothes out of his dresser.

What got into him? I fretted over it while I showered and then quickly dressed. I hadn't washed my hair so it wouldn't be wet.

When I finished, I packed up my things, knowing that even though I didn't want to, I should return to my family.

I came out with my two bags, and Landan noticed them. He looked away, a muscle ticking in his jaw as he did. I frowned and went to stare out the window. What an incredible view. It was one that I would never forget. In fact, there was nothing about this trip that I wanted to forget—including Landan.

"I woke Luna and Marcus up. They are going to come with us."

"Okay, great. Do they have their snow gear?"

He smiled for the first time since we'd had sex this morning. "If you are a skier, you don't go anywhere around here this time of year without it."

"Makes sense."

He pulled out four travel cups, filled them with coffee, and then returned to the stove where he made a large skillet of scrambled eggs.

"Can I help with anything?"

"No, I got this. I will warm up turkey bacon and make wraps before we go."

"Okay," I stated and returned to the window, confused by his behavior. I fretted over it while I stood there and was glad when Luna and Marcus came out of the bedroom.

We ate, and I remained quiet while they talked. Twice, I saw Luna looking between Landan and me with a puzzled look on her face. I shrugged once, not sure what to say.

After we ate, I said I would do the dishes while he checked the gear and loaded Marcus's stuff.

I was alone in the house and frustrated by the tension that had suddenly appeared between us. What could have changed? Everything had been going so well, and I didn't get it.

I was almost to the point of crying when I heard the door from the garage open. I felt hands on my shoulders a moment later as I rinsed a plate in the sink. "I'm sorry."

"What do you have to be sorry for?" I asked.

"For shutting down on you."

I turned, reaching for the dish towel and leaning back against the sink. "Why did you?"

He sighed as he focused out the window. "Because while I was staring at you, I didn't want you to leave. Then I realized I had no right to even suggest you stay. We don't know each other, and—"

I put my fingers over his lips. "Would it be strange to say that at that moment, I was thinking that I never wanted to leave? I didn't want to leave here, and I didn't want to leave you."

"You were?"

"Yes, I was, and then you shut me out, and I wasn't sure what was going on."

He pulled me close and held me. "Coral, I've never felt like this."

"Me either," I stated softly against his chest.

He kissed my brow and pulled back. "Can we talk about this later?"

"I would like that," I replied.

He kissed me once, and then we hustled toward the garage. I went to pick up my two bags, and he looked at me with a silent plea. I set them back down, and he squeezed my hand and led me out of the house.

***

SKIING THAT AFTERNOON WAS INCREDIBLE. I felt more alive and more unrestrained than I had ever felt. The four of us were well matched in our abilities, and we went up and down the slopes as quickly as we could. By the time we finished at four that afternoon, we were all exhausted and starved.

We decided to stay at the resort for dinner and ended up dancing and gathering with other people Luna, Landan, and Marcus knew. By the night's end, I felt like I had a new group of friends.

It was like this was where my life was leading me this whole time. I had trouble picturing myself going home and didn't even want to think about my concerns at the café. They were a world away.

Why had I ever thought I could run a café? My heart was here on the slopes, and now that I had seen Lake Tahoe, I couldn't imagine skiing anywhere else. I could save my pennies and return as often as possible—even if things didn't work out with Landan and me.

We returned to his place late, and I realized that my phone had long since died. I didn't care, though. My family knew who I was with, and I knew that I would have to return to them tomorrow. As much as I wished I could stay hidden away with Landan forever, tomorrow was Thanksgiving.

Both of us needed to be with our families. What bothered me more than anything was wishing I could spend the day with his family, not mine. How wrong was that?

I had more fun with Luna in one day than in a year with my sisters. There was a problem there, and I knew it. Ever since Mom died, I had felt a great chasm between us, and I initially thought that it would eventually get better, but it never did.

After Landan and I made love quietly that night, I curled in his arms and murmured, "I don't want to go back."

He leaned beside my ear, speaking quietly. "You mean to the big house or home?"

I snickered quietly. "Either. Both."

He hugged me tightly, kissing my head. "I know how you feel, although we could sneak away after dinner tomorrow and come back here."

I turned in his arms. "Could we? Would that be wrong?"

He shrugged his shoulder. "Who cares what everyone else thinks? It's what we want. Let's do it."

I grinned at him. "I like that idea."

"Okay, then we have a plan. We can swap cellphone numbers

and keep each other updated when we can make a break for it. Although, I will have to be back early on Friday. I have a meeting with my father that I can't miss."

"Fine," I muttered. "If you must."

He tickled me, and I squealed as I squirmed under the covers. A few minutes later, we snuggled deeply into the covers, and after I heard his breathing deepen, I whispered, "I think I'm falling in love with you."

He surprised me by moving and brushed a kiss to the back of my head, whispering back, "I think I'm falling in love with you too."

I practically squealed with delight, but instead, I pushed back against him and closed my eyes tightly, being happier than I had ever been. For the first time since the trip came about, I was thankful that my family had made me come. That's what I will focus on tomorrow. The fact that they made me take a vacation.

I never expected to enjoy Lake Tahoe like I had, and I certainly didn't expect to meet someone like Landan.

"I DON'T WANT to leave you," I whined as we sat in the driveway beside his parents' house.

"I know, but if you don't, your family will be angry with me for kidnapping you."

"Would you? For real? Would you kidnap me?"

He grinned. "Get out of my truck and go to the guesthouse. I will see you later." He pulled me closer over the console.

"Fine, but that's no fun."

"We can have fun later."

"Can we enjoy the hot tub again?"

"Baby, we can enjoy any part of my house you want as long as we are naked."

"You got yourself a deal," I said, feeling giddy and wanting to skip Thanksgiving dinner and return to his house on the north side of the lake. I couldn't even remember how often we'd had sex, but it wasn't enough.

Forever wouldn't be enough with him.

He met me at the front of the truck, kissed me again, held my hand, and walked me to the path between the houses. "Text me later and keep me updated on time."

"I will," I walked backward, not wanting to stop looking at him.

"Turn around before you slip," he said, shaking his head as I started doing just that.

"Okay, fine! Stop standing there looking so sexy."

"Wait, get back here. I changed my mind!"

"Nope," I said sassily, "It's too late." I waved my fingers at him and then turned around and began skipping toward the front of the house. I heard him laughing, and when I reached the corner, I glanced back to see him shaking his head and waving again.

God, I was crazy about that guy. Neither of us had mentioned the words we said last night, but they were front and center in my mind as I climbed the steps and pushed open the door. Nothing could ruin my mood!

Not until Carmen and Candy rushed toward me. "Where the hell have you been?" Carmen demanded. "We've been trying to reach you for hours."

"What's the big deal? You act like the world is falling down."

"Not the world, only Dad," Carmen growled.

"What?"

"Dad fell on the ice, Coral. We have been trying to call you for hours. That was so irresponsible of you!" Candy snapped.

And just like that, my incredible mood burst like a pin into a balloon. Once again, I had let my family down and was being hailed as the family failure.

CHAPTER SIXTEEN

LANDAN

The last few days had been the best days of my life. Who would have thought that the woman I saw staring over the lake would have touched so many parts of my soul? I sure hadn't. I began to miss her the minute she disappeared around the corner of the guesthouse.

It was so damn weird that as I let myself into the house, I wondered if she was a witch and had somehow cast a spell on me without me knowing. Was it possible? Did witches exist?

"Oh man, he lives!" Leo said as he came down the steps and saw me. "I was getting worried about you. Glad you came up for air."

"Funny, man, very funny."

I followed him into the kitchen. "What's going on? Did I miss anything?"

"Oh, there you are, Landan. I tried to call you, but it went to voicemail."

I pulled my phone out, noting a few missed calls. "Sorry, I forgot I had it on silent. What did you need?"

"It wasn't something I needed; Coral's family was looking for her."

"They knew where she was."

"Yes, but her father had an accident, and they were trying to contact her."

A tendril of anxiety whipped through my system. "What do you mean an accident? Is he okay?"

"I think so. He's home now, but they took him to the hospital after he slipped on the ice. They were worried he might have broken a hip or something."

I started to pull up Coral's contact information, but my mother put her hand on my wrist. "Leave her alone to deal with this. I am sure she will reach out to you a bit later. I know her family was upset that she couldn't be reached."

"I should go over and apologize."

"No, you should get in the kitchen and help me. You know that you make the best stuffing."

"Fine," I replied, turning the volume of my phone up to the highest setting so I wouldn't miss a call or message from Coral.

"What were you two doing? Luna said that she stayed at your place with Marcus. They didn't interrupt you two, did they?"

"They got stuck in the storm. We had a great time. We soaked in the hot tub, had a nice dinner, and even played a game of Scrabble during the storm. Then we got up and hit the slopes."

"I hear Coral is quite the skier."

"She is. I was happily surprised to see someone who could keep up with us. You know we are lunatics on the slopes. She's just as bad—or good, depending on how you look at it."

"Does she ski as well as Luna?"

"Probably a little bit better. Coral worked on the ski patrol during and after college."

"Oh, so she has a lot of experience," Mom said with a warm smile. "I'm glad she was evenly matched for you."

"She is," I said quietly, thinking about how great of a match she was, as I started to break apart pieces of bread for the stuffing.

"How well did you two get along?" my mother asked as Laney stepped into the room, looking like she needed a few more hours of sleep. She was wearing a hoodie and had it pulled over her head. Her long brown hair hung out below her chin.

"You look hung over," I commented as she went straight to the coffee pot without even a hello.

"Yeah, something like that," Laney said.

Mom and I shared a look, and Mom raised a brow as if to ask me if I knew what was going on. I had no clue. Of all my siblings, Laney and I probably spent the least time talking. Most of the time, she was moody and kept to herself. She seemed content to sit on the sidelines and watch the interactions of everyone else.

"Where have you been?" she asked after a sip and curling up on a chair near the table.

"I was at my house."

"We aren't good enough for you?" Laney said a bit snidely.

"No, I was entertaining a guest."

She pursed her lips, looking out the window for a moment. "I didn't know you were seeing someone."

"I'm not, or at least I wasn't."

"Landan was spending time with Coral Winston. He was showing her around the lake area."

Laney nodded, got up, collected her coffee mug, and left the room, muttering something about returning to bed.

Mom sighed a few moments after she left. "I'm not sure what's going on with her. She seems even more withdrawn than normal."

"Do you want me to talk to her?"

"I don't think it will work. I asked Lance to do so, and he

tried, but she said she was fine and didn't want to share anything with him."

I frowned. "Maybe I can reach her, or you could ask Luna to try."

"If anyone can get Laney to talk, it will probably be Lily."

"Then ask her to speak to her."

"I will," she replied with a wearier sigh. "You know it stresses me out when you all aren't doing well."

"Well, at least you don't have to worry about me."

She smiled at me as she peeled a potato. "No, I'm glad that I don't, but you did have me worried for a while after you and Eve split up."

"I just needed a little while to get over it."

"Are you over it now?"

"Yes. I got over it a while ago, and after spending this time with Coral, I realized that it never would have worked with Eve and me in the first place."

"Why is that?"

"Because I finally recognized how selfish Eve was and how she didn't appreciate what I did."

"Does Coral appreciate it?"

I couldn't help but grin. "Coral is the complete opposite of Eve. She's up and dressed in twenty minutes, and that's with taking a shower. She's down-to-earth, loves to laugh and joke around, and she'd prefer to curl up on the couch and watch a movie instead of hitting the bar."

"Sounds like you two do have a lot in common."

"We do." I paused and grew slightly nervous as I tried to form the words I wanted to ask my mother. "Um, how did you know that Dad was the one?"

My mother stopped peeling for a moment but didn't look my way. She continued working on the potato as she said, "I knew the moment I met your father that he was my future. It just felt right. It was like I had a piece of a puzzle missing, and the moment I met him, it clicked into place."

"So, it was love at first sight?"

"No, I can't say that I loved him at first sight, but I sure did like him enough."

"How long did it take you to know you loved him?"

This time, she set the potato and peeler down and turned to me, wiping her hands on a towel. "Are you asking because you are interested in how your father and I fell in love, or are you asking because you feel like you might be having those feelings toward Coral?"

"I might be having those feelings toward Coral," I stated without hesitation.

The smile she gave me looked almost sad. "I saw a change in you the first night you met her after you came back from skiing. Your eyes lit up when you talked about the fun you had with her that day." She set the towel down and leanded against the counter beside me. "Luna said she saw a lot of sparks between you two."

"Yes, there are."

"Are you sure it's not the sparks you feel instead of love?"

"I don't know. I'm not sure that I have ever felt anything like this before. It's more than sparks. It's this almost *need* to be near her, to see her smile, to touch her and listen to her laugh. When you told me her father was hurt, the first thing I wanted to do was make sure she was okay and see if there was anything I could do."

"What about the fact that she lives on the other side of the country?"

"That I haven't figured out yet, although I know how much she loves it here. She was saying last night that she didn't want to leave."

"This place is magical to some people."

"I know. Coral feels the magic, Mom. Sometimes, I look at her, and she is so absorbed in the view out the window that she seems like she is lost in it. Like she's trying to memorize every aspect of what she sees."

"Maybe she is. Maybe she knows this might be the last time she sees it, and she never wants to forget it."

"Oh, I have a feeling she will be back."

"Did she say that?"

"Well, we talked about her coming back in the summer so we could go out on the water."

"That is something to look forward to."

"It is, but I'm not sure I want to wait seven or eight months for her to return."

"You could always visit her."

"I could. I'd like to. It would be fun to see where she lives. She suggested I come out, and she could take me to the mountains she likes to ski at, but they are a lot smaller than here."

"No place is as great as Lake Tahoe for skiing," my mother said with a grin.

"No, I agree with you there."

"I am sure you two will figure something out."

"I hope so, Mom."

She touched my arm. "I hope you do, too, Landan. I want you to be happy and have a family."

"Coral can't have kids." I blurted the words, and my mother's brow lifted.

"Well, that's a heavy subject to have when you two are just getting to know one another."

"We were talking about what we wanted out of life. She had an accident when she was younger and had to have a hysterectomy."

"I am very sorry to hear that, and if anyone understands that, it's me."

"I know you do, Mom. That's why I said something."

"Is she open to adoption?"

"She is."

"Good. If you two reach that point, I can tell you exactly where to go." She patted my arm and turned back to the counter. "Because one of these days, I would like to have a grandchild to spoil. It amazes me that with eight children, mostly in their thirties with careers and such, not one of you has a kid."

"That we know of." I laughed, and she joined me.

"Yes, that is true. You boys do have a habit of sowing your oats quite often."

I laughed loudly. "Hey, not me! You're talking about Lucas and Lance."

"Yes, those are the two I worry about the most."

"Well, don't worry about them, Mom. One day, you will have that first grandchild."

"I hope so. Your father and I aren't getting any younger, you know."

"If I could give you one tomorrow, I would."

She chuckled. "You know it's not like you can go to the store and buy one."

"You did. You bought four."

She gave me a dramatically annoyed look, but I knew she was joking. "I did not buy your siblings. I rescued them."

"Who did you rescue?" Leo asked as he stepped into the room.

"You, but it's too bad you're a lost cause," I said to him with a smirk.

"Funny." He slapped me on the back. "You are so damn funny."

After that, the rest of the family—except Laney—came into the kitchen, and the conversation moved from my love life and children to many other things as we all helped with something for Thanksgiving dinner.

My father reminded me that we had a meeting early tomorrow morning. We were trying to wrap up a deal with a Canadian company, but things were going awry, and we needed to nail things down. The deal was worth one hundred million, and none of us wanted to screw this one up.

CHAPTER SEVENTEEN

CORAL

I stared at my sisters. "Is he okay?"

"No, he's not okay," Candy hissed. "He fell and got stitches on his head."

Carmen put her hand on Candy's arm. "He is fine. Yes, he got a few stitches, but it is no big deal. We were more worried that he might have broken a hip or something, but they said he was fine. He needs to take it easy because they aren't sure if he has a concussion, but otherwise, he will be all right."

If he would be fine, why were they freaking out on me? "Where is he?"

"Lying on the couch," Carmen said as Candy shook her head and walked away as if disgusted. What the hell was her problem?

I shifted around Carmen and headed toward the living room, or what I thought was the living room. It was empty, so I went to another room and found him lying on the couch with his eyes closed and his hands folded over his lap. I froze. That pose was so similar to how my mother had been the last time I had seen her. The room around me spun, and I threw a hand to the side to balance on the back of a nearby chair. I must have made a noise because his eyes snapped open.

"Coral, honey, you're back." His voice didn't appear angry with me for not being here, which I was glad.

"Hey, Dad, I'm so sorry I wasn't here when you fell."

"Nonsense, everyone is making a big deal out of nothing. No one would have batted an eye if I had fallen at home. They sure wouldn't have reacted like they all did."

I sat down, realizing that everyone had blown this out of proportion. "I'm glad you are okay."

"The worst part was banging my head. I have a headache and a few threads holding my head back together. It's no big deal."

"You're sure you are all right?"

He took my hand. "I am more than all right. Tell me what you have been up to. I heard you were with one of the Lancaster boys."

"Dad, he's about to turn forty. I don't think you can call him a boy."

"You know what I meant." He smiled tenderly. "What were you two doing, or do I not want to know?"

I laughed, feeling better for the first time since I entered the room.

"Landan took me around the lake and showed me some awesome things. Dad, you should see the north side of the lake. If you think it is beautiful down here, it is astounding on the Nevada side."

I told him all—well, not all—the things we had done, and he listened with avid interest as I went along. Eventually, Silvia joined us and asked tons of questions.

When I got done, I could tell my father needed to rest. He looked tired, and when he blinked, it took longer for his lids to reopen.

"Dad, why don't you rest? I will see what I can help with in the kitchen."

"I think that's a good idea," Silvia seconded my suggestion.

"I believe I could use a nap," my father said, and I frowned as I turned away. My father rarely napped, and hearing that at ten in the morning worried me. Silvia followed me from the room after kissing him, and I stopped her in the hallway.

"Is he really all right, Silvia?"

"He will be fine. He bumped his head harder than he wanted to admit, but he has a hard head. We all know that. The doctors said he will probably be more tired than usual for a few days and should rest when he feels tired."

"But he will be okay?" I needed to know that this vacation wouldn't kill my father. I could not imagine the guilt I would feel if it did.

"Don't worry about your father." She took my arm and led me away. "What I want to hear are the juicy details of your time with Landan."

I chuckled. "Juicy? Who said they were juicy?"

She gave me a pointed look. "I wasn't born yesterday, Coral. You are both adults, and it was obvious there is chemistry between you two."

I put my head next to hers. "Between me and you, there is a lot of chemistry between us."

She giggled. "And that's what I want to hear about."

We sat on the front porch by the firepit and looked out over the lake as we talked more about my time with Landan.

"I do believe someone is smitten."

"Yeah, I am. Is it that obvious?"

"Well, since I have known you, I have never seen your eyes so bright or your smile so wide. I'm happy for you, but what will you do when you go home?"

I deflated. "I have no clue. I have a business to run back home, and he lives here. I'm not sure there could be a future for us."

"If it is meant to be, you two will figure it out."

"I hope so, Silvia, I really do."

I DIDN'T REACH out to Landan until after four that afternoon. After speaking with Silvia, Riley and Evan joined us on the porch, and eventually, the whole family, including my father, was sitting around the fire, laughing and sharing stories. For the first time in a long time, I enjoyed being with my family, and even though I would think of Landan occasionally, I knew that I needed to give my family the attention they deserved.

I sent Landan a message a few minutes before we sat down to eat. *We are getting ready to eat. I hope you are having a great day.*

A few minutes later, he replied. *We just finished, and I am stuffed to the brim. I'm sorry to hear about your dad. Is he okay?*

He is alright. He has a few stitches on his head, and he's tired, but he is in good spirits. However, I'm not sure if I can get away tonight.

I completely understand. Maybe we can hang out for a little while later. Get our families together to play a game or something.

I will approach the subject with everyone over dinner. Talk to you later.

It was a long moment before I got a response, but it made me smile like a fool when I saw it. *Is it weird that I miss you, even though I know you are right next door?*

No, I miss you too. I can't imagine how hard it will be when I go home.

Yeah, we need to discuss that.

Later. We need to put food on the table. XOXO

XOXOXOXO right back at you.

OVER DINNER, I laughed and joked along with everyone else, and

Ethan was the one to comment on my good mood. "About time you got laid. You are much more fun to be around now."

"Hey!" I barked at him. "That's not nice."

"But it's true," Evan said with a grin.

Everyone nodded, and I chuckled and shook my head. "Whatever."

"Are you going to keep in touch with him when you return home?" Alaina asked.

It was one thing to have a heart-to-heart about how I felt with Silvia and quite another to discuss it with my siblings. I didn't think they deserved to know what was happening in my love life. They sure never shared what was happening in theirs with me.

I shrugged a shoulder and filled my fork. "We haven't discussed it."

Which was true; we hadn't discussed it. Personally, I didn't see how it could work, and that thought depressed me, but if there was a will, there was a way.

"Well, I am glad you are having a vacation fling," Carmen said. "Maybe once you get home and realize that your café is still standing, you can find time to enjoy yourself and start dating again."

The thought of dating anyone who wasn't Landan made me slightly ill. "Who said I was going to date anyone?"

Candy looked at me like I had two heads. "Are you telling me that after having sex a couple of times, you aren't dying to get back out there? I can't imagine going as long as you have."

"First off, you have no idea how long it has been, Candy. Second, I have no intention of dating anyone when I get home. Landan and I have things to discuss."

Evan wiped his mouth. "You aren't seriously thinking that you two could have something, are you?"

"And why not?" I asked.

"Because he lives out here, and you live in Pennsylvania. The guy sells multimillion-dollar companies, and you own this rinky-dink coffee shop."

I saw red. "Says the man who is a nurse and married a billionaire."

"My situation is different," he started, and Alaina touched his arm.

"Leave Coral alone. She is right, and I think it is great that Landan and she are getting along."

He looked instantly contrite. "You're right."

After that, the conversation moved off me, and I withdrew back into myself, eagerly getting up once everyone finished eating and I started to clear the table. I wanted nothing more than to escape the house and see Landan.

I sent him a message. *You free?*

For you, absolutely. Are we going to get together with your siblings?

No, they have plans. It will just be me, is that okay?

Absolutely. Come over when you are ready.

While everyone was hustling around, I helped clean up in the kitchen, and then I went to find my father. "Dad, do you mind if I spend time with Landan at his house?"

He held my hand. "Go enjoy yourself, and I'm sorry your brothers and sisters are being so difficult."

"It's okay, Dad. I'm used to it now."

"That doesn't mean they should behave that way. Go have fun, and I'll see you in the morning. Are you going to stay over there tonight?"

"Would you be upset if I did?"

"No, enjoy the time that you have with him. You deserve it, sweetheart."

"I love you, Daddy."

"I love you too, Coral."

I collected my jacket and slipped out the door without

anyone seeing me. I made sure to be careful of my footing on the way over. I didn't want to be the next one to fall.

I knocked on the door and heard laughter coming from inside. The door opened, and Luna pulled me in. "She's here! Thank God! I will have someone on my side now!"

Within seconds, I was enveloped in the family as we sat down to play a game, and they felt more like family than mine had tonight.

Several hours later, Lucy, Landan's mom, put her hand on my shoulder. "Good night, Coral. Will we see you for breakfast?"

Landan chuckled. "That's her way of asking if you are staying the night."

"If you don't mind, I'd love that."

"You are more than welcome to join us." She surprised me by leaning down and kissing my cheek. "See you in the morning."

I blinked back unexpected tears as she left the room, and Landan tucked me close to my side and kissed my forehead. "She likes you almost as much as I like you."

I dropped my eyes as emotion overtook me, and he lifted my chin and turned my face toward him. "You okay?"

"Yeah, just a little overwhelmed. It's been a long day."

"Want to go upstairs?'

"No, let's stay here a little longer. I want to finish the game."

"Your wish is my command, my dear." Landan winked.

"Come on, you two, cut out the sexy talk," Levi taunted us, and Landan threw a wadded-up napkin toward him.

Then we returned to the game, and my heart felt like it would burst with love for this man and his family.

CHAPTER EIGHTEEN

LANDAN

We went to bed late; luckily, my alarm didn't wake Coral in the morning. I slipped out of bed, put on a button-down shirt, and went down to meet with my father for the video conference call we were doing with the clients.

"How are you today, son?" He stood at the coffee pot.

"I'm great, Dad. How about you?" He poured a second cup of coffee and pushed it toward me.

"I'd be better if this deal went through, but having everyone together this week was nice."

"Yeah, it was."

"I guess meeting Coral was a bonus for you."

"Yes, very much so. I never expected to meet anyone anytime soon."

"She leaves on Sunday?"

"Yes," I told him.

He pursed his lips. "I might need you to head out to Quebec tomorrow. Is that going to be a problem?"

The last thing I wanted to do was miss one second with Coral, but I couldn't tell my father no. This client had been waffling for a while. I knew that if things didn't go well today, one of us would need to speak to them face-to-face, and Dad was leaving for Tokyo on Sunday.

"Of course, it won't be a problem," I told him as I went to sit at the table. I wondered how hard it would be to fly to Pennsylvania after the meeting. Maybe I could tell Coral that I would come to see her home. Or perhaps I should surprise her. That might be better. Tim could give me the information that I would need.

My father sat beside me. "By the way, happy birthday."

I smirked. "I can't believe I am officially forty years old."

"You're catching up to me," he smirked.

"You still have twenty-two years on me, old man."

He shook his head. "Better watch that old man shit. Won't be long until you are where I am."

I sighed. "Yeah, I know."

He glanced at his watch. "All right, let's take care of this so we can at least enjoy your birthday party today."

I WASN'T happy when the meeting was over because it solidified the fact that I would need to travel to Quebec, and not only that, but then I would have to fly to British Columbia, which was on the opposite side of Canada. It would not be easy to make a stop in Pennsylvania. I would have to fly from one side of the country to another and then back again to see her.

I went into the kitchen while my father called his secretary to get her started on the new documents I would need to deliver in person.

My mom, Luna, and Leo were in the kitchen. "Did Coral get up yet?"

"She did, and she said she would talk to you later. She returned to the guesthouse to shower and change."

"Okay, good. I'm have to run up to my place and get a bag packed. I have to fly to Quebec tomorrow."

Mom shook her head. "You guys couldn't fix things over the phone?"

"No, they want us to kiss their asses and have the new deal hand-delivered." I sighed. "But I expected that. They want to discuss it on Sunday, and then if it is good, they will sign it, and I will have to deliver it to their British Columbia office personally."

"When is Coral's family leaving?" Leo asked.

"Sunday," I stated.

"That sucks," Leo grunted before he shoved a muffin into his mouth.

"Yes, it does. I'm going to go up and change. What time is the party today?"

"Six."

"Okay, then I will make sure I am back by five to help with anything you need."

My mom stood. "No, you arrive at five forty-five in time to greet your guests. I don't want you doing anything today." She came to stand in front of me. "I can't believe my firstborn is forty. How did you get so old?"

"Not just your firstborn, but your favorite," I teased.

"You know that I love each of you the same," she said with a shake of her head.

Of course, she told each of us privately that we were her favorite, which I didn't mind. I knew she had enough love for all of us, and at times, I am sure that one of us stuck out more than the others. Today would be my day to be her favorite because it was my birthday.

"I know you do." I kissed her cheek.

On my way up to my room, I sent Coral a text. *Want to run up to my place with me?*

I didn't get an answer from her for a few minutes, but finally, as I was heading downstairs, she replied. *When are you leaving?*

Depends on if you are coming with me.

Can you give me about twenty minutes? I just got out of the shower.

Sure, I will even give you thirty if you need the extra time.

See you in fifteen, Coral replied quickly, and I knew that she meant it. I loved that she was quick to get dressed and didn't need to fuss over her appearance. It had been a long time since I dated someone like that. Wait, had I ever dated someone like that? Maybe in college, but not as an adult.

Sixteen minutes later, there was a knock on the front door, and I opened it, peering at my watch. "You're late. You said fifteen, and it's been sixteen."

She mock glared at me. "By one minute, and you said you were giving me thirty minutes."

"No." I leaned forward and kissed her as she stepped in. "I said I would give you thirty if you needed it."

"Then I am early because I only needed sixteen. That last minute was me walking over here carefully so I didn't face-plant on the icy path."

I frowned momentarily. "I need to remind Lance and Levi to put salt down. We don't need anyone else falling. How is your dad, by the way?"

"He looks better today. Yesterday, he looked so tired."

"Good, I'm glad to hear he is doing better. Let me grab my keys, and we can go."

Luna and Lily came down the stairs and both hugged Coral as they joined us in the foyer.

Luna joked, "Just can't get enough of him, can you?"

"We only have two more days, so I want every second I can get," Coral said perkily.

Luna glanced at me, and I knew she was aware that I was

going to Canada and just realized that I hadn't said anything yet. I shook my head to answer her unspoken question.

"Well, you two need to get out of here so you can enjoy every moment you have."

I collected my keys as Coral said hello to my mom, and then we slipped into the garage. I was putting off telling her I had to leave and didn't say anything until we reached my house.

"There was a reason I had to come by my house."

"Yeah, what's that?" she asked as she wrapped her arms around my waist. "You wanted to get me in bed again?"

"Coral, I most definitely want to get you back in my bed, but that's not why I needed to come here."

"Okay, why?"

"I have to fly to Canada tomorrow."

She stared at me, and I saw the moment she realized what I was saying. "And I won't see you after tonight."

I shook my head and held her close. "I'm sorry, but this deal is too important for me to put off."

"I get it. Work comes first." She held on to me like I was about to walk out the door now. "How long will you be gone?"

"I don't know, but I'll be in Quebec for a few days, and then I need to fly to British Columbia. Originally, it was just going to be Quebec, and I thought about surprising you by flying down to see your home on my way back, but it's not feasible now. I would be crossing the continent four times."

"No, that's too much." She leaned back and gave me a tender smile. "But I appreciate you even thinking about that. It would have been nice, but to be honest, when I get home, things are going to be hectic. I wouldn't be able to give you much of my time."

"Then we will plan something else." I took hold of her face, leaning closer to her. "I will come to see you, but we can plan it so you can take some time off and show me around. Hopefully, you can show me your favorite slopes."

"I can try to do that, but I can't promise anything right now, Landan. Some things are up in the air, and I'm not sure what I will need to do."

"Well, if I can help at all, you let me know."

"I appreciate that, but I need to deal with this." She stepped up on her toes. "Enough talking. If I only have you for a few more hours, we need to make the best of it."

"Did I tell you how incredible you are?"

"No."

I swooped her into my arms. "Well, you are, Coral. I am so glad that I met you."

"And I'm glad I met you."

I carried her into the bedroom, and we stayed there for a few hours before we were both starving, and I needed to get packed. After a light meal, she lay on the bed and watched me pack my suitcase. Because I would be gone for more than a couple of days, and these were important meetings, I needed to pack a larger bag and bring several suits.

"I bet you look pretty snazzy in those suits," she commented as I folded them to fit.

"I guess I don't look too bad."

"I'm sure you don't. I wonder how many women drool over you when you walk past."

I laughed. "Hardly."

"You don't think you are handsome?"

"I guess I'm all right. I think most women find the money my family has more attractive than me."

She frowned. "See, that irks me. I can't imagine being with someone because of how much money they have. I want to love them for who they are, and I want them to love me for who I am."

"So, you don't care that I'm a millionaire?"

"Nope, Alaina is a billionaire, and it doesn't impress me all that much. Don't get me wrong. I would love to be able to afford everything that my heart desires, but I don't need it. My house is full of hand-me-downs and thrift shop finds, and I'm happy with that."

"You are amazing, Coral. There are so few people like you in the world."

"Aw, shucks!" She began to blush, and I dropped the shirt in my hand and tackled her to the bed as she laughed. "What are you doing? Your shirt is going to be all wrinkled."

"That's what irons are for."

She ran her hand over my face. "I don't even own an iron."

I raised my eyebrows.. "You don't own an iron?"

"No, I prefer to wear my clothes wrinkled. I think it goes better with my personality."

I barked out a laugh and kissed her hard. "You are amazing."

"I aim to please," she said in a sassy voice.

"Don't I know that. You have been pleasing me up one side and down the other all week." I grew quiet. "I really am glad that I met you, Coral. You are more incredible than I could have imagined."

"I'm glad I met you too, Landan, and thank you for sharing this with me. You made it even more special."

"Well, you deserved to feel special."

My phone beeped, and I looked at it. "Shit, we need to get going soon. I promised my mom I would be home by five forty-five to greet guests. It wouldn't look right if the guest of honor wasn't there for his fortieth birthday party."

"No, I guess it wouldn't." She looked sad and then sat up on the edge of the bed. "Can I stay with you again tonight?"

"I would love nothing else, but I have to leave at four-thirty to get to Reno to catch my flight."

"That's okay. I can get up with you and kiss you goodbye."

I leaned over and kissed her once more. "Not goodbye, Coral. Kiss me to wish me luck and to hold me over until I see you again in a few weeks."

CHAPTER NINETEEN

CORAL

I was devastated that he was leaving and our time was being cut short, but it wasn't fair to make him feel bad about it. He had an important job, and it came first. My feelings came second.

I kept as upbeat as possible, and on the way back to his parents' house, he held my hand tightly on the console between us. I studied him as we drove, observing intently how his wavy hair fell past his ears, the shape of his jaw, and the curve of his nose and chin.

My heart clenched as I realized I was head over heels in love with this man. How could that even be possible? I knew my parents hadn't known each other long, but they didn't fall in love in only a few days.

I had never believed in love at first sight, and even though Evan and Alaina had fallen quickly for one another, and Carmen and Tim had known that they still loved each other after only a short time, I still wasn't sure it was possible.

Were the feelings that I was having for Landan merely lust? No, these feelings in me were not something I had ever experienced before. This wasn't just because I found him attractive or that we shared chemistry. Landan and I shared more than that. We shared pieces of our hearts and souls.

When we arrived at his parents' house, I told him I'd see him in a little while so I could change before I came over. Most of my siblings were already dressed and ready to go, and I didn't mind them going over before me. I had already given him his present, not that it was much of a present. The only thing I had to give was my heart and my body. It's not like I had time to go shopping or even knew what he might need or want.

As I changed clothes and touched up my makeup, I realized that while we had shared and talked a lot, we still didn't know each other very well. Had we met in my hometown, would we have had such a connection? Perhaps it was just the magic of Lake Tahoe that brought us together. Or the love of skiing. What else did we have in common?

As I headed to his house, I saw a lot of cars, and most of them were ones that I could never afford. For the first time since I met him, I felt slightly uncomfortable as I stepped into the house and glanced around. Streamers hung everywhere, and giant colorful mylar balloons bounced in the corners. Over fifty people milled about, and it was only a few minutes after six. How many people did this man know?

I scanned the crowd, finding him on the other side of the living room area, where he was talking to a group of people. He wore charcoal-gray slacks and a light-gray sweater. On his wrist was a dress watch he hadn't worn earlier. Without even being close, I knew what he wore was expensive, and the wristwatch was probably a Rolex or something comparable.

I wore a watch, too, but it was a Timex. My dress was from a discount store and probably cost not even half of what his sweater cost. What was I doing with a man like him?

It was the first time his wealth made me feel uncomfortable and I glanced down at my dress and slightly scuffed boots. I gnawed on my bottom lip as a striking woman approached him, lifting her face and kissing his lips. I froze. Who was she? A previous girlfriend? Was that Eve, his ex-fiancée?

Luna suddenly appeared at my side. "Don't get yourself in a bother. That's Tia. They have been like best friends since middle school. She's like a sister to him."

"Oh," I replied, glancing her way. "Was it that obvious?"

She giggled softly. "Only to those watching you."

"Well, thanks for letting me know. I'm not usually the jealous type."

She shrugged. "I get it. When you find that one whom you think is the one, it's hard not to get jealous."

I turned to her, studying her face. "What makes you think he's the one for me?"

She rolled her eyes. "Oh, please! You two have been gaga over each other since you first saw one another. All of us can see it." She glanced around. "I wasn't a big fan of Eve. I didn't like her from the moment I met her, and I always told Landan. He told me to keep my opinions to myself. You I knew I liked in a matter of minutes. Besides, the change that has come over him in mere days is amazing."

"Thank you, Luna. I appreciate that."

"Now, why don't you get over there and spend what time you can with him."

I hugged her. "Your words mean a lot to me, Luna. They really do."

She pulled back and grinned at me. "How you feel for my brother means a lot to me."

Without another word, Luna strolled away, and I made a beeline to Landan.

"There you are," he said happily as I appeared at his side. He glanced down my body and took my hands. "You look beautiful."

I laughed a little nervously. Perhaps Landan didn't care that my dress cost me about thirty dollars off a clearance rack at

Marshall's. If he didn't care, why should I? "Thank you," I responded politely, peering at the two men and one woman around him as he tucked me close to his side.

"This is Coral Winston. Her family is visiting Lake Tahoe and staying in our guesthouse," Landan told the other guests.

"Are you enjoying your visit?" the older woman asked.

"I am. I have never been here before, and the skiing has been amazing."

"You are lucky. We have had a lot of snow already this year. Usually, the heavier snows don't come until December, but we started getting them in October." One of the men continued. "It's going to be another huge year. What did we have, seventy or eighty feet last year by the time spring officially hit us?"

The woman replied, "I think it was just over eighty."

We continued to discuss skiing a bit longer, and the woman eyed Landan and me closely, smiling as if she were happy to see him with someone. That, in turn, made me happy, and the night whizzed by faster than I had hoped for.

Landan kept me at his side, introducing me to everyone who approached him as we went from room to room. There must have been over two hundred people in the house, and yet it didn't seem crowded until it was time to cut the cake, and most people gathered in the large living room or stood on the stairs or balcony above to sing and watch.

I was awestruck that a man like Landan could be interested in me, the reality of how important and wealthy he was finally hitting me. Until now, he was just Landan, a man who loved to ski and stare at the incredible scenery around us and could make my body scream for things it didn't even realize it wanted.

Yet, he was so much more. He was a loved sibling, a devoted friend, and a handsome and debonair businessman. What was he doing with me? How could he possibly be interested in someone so simple and plain when he had all these beautiful women to pick from.

Unfortunately, as I returned from the restroom, I realized the answer.

I paused a few feet away, hidden behind several blue and green mylar balloons. In front of me, Landan was talking to Evan, Ethan, and Tim.

Evan slapped him on the shoulder. "Landan, I really appreciate you spending so much time with Coral. She needed a good time, and you gave her exactly what she needed."

"It wasn't hard." Landan laughed, and my heart fell. Had they asked him to spend time with me? Help me have a good time? Is that why he had been so nice to me? So willing to spend every minute with me? Was I merely a charity case?

Ethan spoke, "You have given her some great memories. I can't thank you enough for that. We owe you. You let us know what you want, and we will find a way to get it for you."

I thought I would vomit as I put my hand to my stomach and stepped back into the shadows. What happened to all those words about how he felt so much for me and would miss me? What about the fact that he said I was different and wanted me to come back to see him? Had it all been a lie? Had Tim and my siblings set this all up that first night? Is that why Landan came over to the house?

I could just imagine Ethan, Riley, Evan, Alaina, Tim, and Carmen talking behind my back about how they needed to find someone to seduce me and keep me busy.

I hustled toward an exit—any exit I could find—and bumped into Silvia just before I reached it. "Coral, are you okay? You look ill."

"I'm not feeling very well. I think something I ate is bothering me. I am going to head back to the house. Can you tell Landan I'm sorry, but I need to go lie down?"

"Absolutely," Silvia said. "Do you want me to come with you?"

"No, no, please stay and enjoy the party."

"Okay, if you need something, your father is resting in bed, and I won't be much longer."

"Thanks, Silvia." I rushed out of the house before I broke down in tears and walked as quickly as I dared on the slick pathway between the houses. As I entered the house, the tears began to slip down my cheeks, and I ran up the stairs to my room.

I paced back and forth, wringing my hands. How dare my siblings do that to me! How dare Landan do that to me! I thought he cared about me! What a fool I was! I bet he hooked up with tourists all the time—a new one every week. Everything he said was a complete lie!

I pulled out my laptop and quickly figured out how to book a flight out of here. Then I packed all my things as fast as I could. Before I left, I stepped onto the balcony. I could hear laughter and music from next door, but I didn't turn to look at that. I took a few seconds to stare at the darkened lake, noting the bright stars in the clear sky and lights shining from homes that dotted the opposite side of the lake.

I thought this place had been magic, but instead, it had been an evil deception. Or perhaps I had been so overwhelmed by the beauty of it, and that allowed them to deceive me easily. I had been right to wonder how someone as incredible and worldly as Landan would be interested in small-town nothing me.

I turned back and gathered my things, and as quietly as I could, I went down the stairs. I hesitated before I left, wondering if I should say something to my father, but decided he would only worry more, so I grabbed a set of keys from the kitchen counter and hustled out to one of the rental SUVs. They could figure out how to get everyone back to the airport on their own. It wasn't my problem.

I pulled out of the driveway and drove down the road, pulling into an empty parking lot before I set up my GPS. I didn't want to chance anyone finding me. I was too emotional and humiliated to have run into anyone else.

Once done, I forced myself to focus on the road and not replay the moments I had spent with Landan. I could shed my tears later. Right now, I had to get out of here. Tears began to blur my vision as my phone gave me a notification. I didn't try to look at it, though. It was night, and I was emotional and on curvy roads that could be icy.

I made it to the highway and then eventually into Reno. I didn't think twice as I took the rental car to the return lot and handed them the keys. I glanced at my tiny watch. I had enough time to get in, check my bag, and run to my gate. Luckily, the Reno airport wasn't that big.

I arrived at the gate to find they had already started boarding and only had to wait a few minutes before my zone was announced. It was a drastic change sitting in the rear of the plane, in the center seat, from when I had flown out to Lake Tahoe in an elegant private plane with gold-plated accents and heated leather seats that fully reclined with footrests.

I felt my phone vibrate and forgot that I had gotten a notification earlier. I pulled out my phone and took a deep breath.

I had three messages. One was from Silvia asking where I had disappeared to. Another was Carmen asking where I was, and the last was from Landan, who wanted to come over to check on me. I didn't respond to any of them and instead turned my phone to airplane mode and slipped it into my purse.

As I closed my eyes, the memories began to overwhelm me, and I sat back and let the tears slide silently down my face. I didn't try to stop them, and I didn't care if anyone saw them.

Just hours before, I was wondering if it was possible to find love at first sight, and now I was wondering how my heart could hurt this much from the betrayal of not only Landan, but my family as well. They had asked him to spend time with me, to show me a good time! How dare they do that! How dare

Landan betray my heart that way. I had been so open and honest with him; it had meant nothing to him.

The older woman in the window seat handed me a small pack of tissues. Without a word, I took them, dabbed at my face, and blew my nose. Then I stared out the window as we took off, saying goodbye to the fantasy of Landan and me and any idiotic fantasy that I had created of a happily ever after.

CHAPTER TWENTY

LANDAN

C oral had excused herself to use the restroom while I was chatting with a few more people. Evan, Ethan, and Tim approached me as I finished with them.

Evan spoke as he slapped me on the shoulder. "Landan, I really appreciate you spending so much time with Coral. She needed a good time, and you gave her exactly what she needed."

"It wasn't hard," I replied. They had no clue how much I had enjoyed spending every moment with her.

Ethan spoke, "You have given her some great memories. I can't thank you enough for that. We owe you. You let us know what you want, and we will find a way to get it for you."

I looked between them. "Why are you thanking me? I'm the lucky one to have run into her."

"Yeah, but you have no clue how hard it has been to pull her away from work. She never hangs out; she doesn't even join in our text conversations," Evan stated.

Tim slapped his arm. "That's because she wasn't even part of the group chat. Did you even bother to check?"

I glanced between Evan and Ethan. "You had a group chat with your other siblings and forgot to add Coral? That's pretty damn lame," I stated, remembering her telling me about it. Suddenly, I felt angrier than I had a right to feel. "That's not just lame, it's pretty fucking rude."

"Whoa!" Evan stated. "It's not like we did it on purpose. Coral works so much, and we only see her on Sunday afternoons for dinner or if we go into the coffee shop."

"Do you ever try to involve her?"

"Of course, we do," Ethan stated firmly. "She is the one who doesn't have time for us."

I clenched my jaw and ground my teeth for a moment. I could not imagine doing that to one of my siblings, even Laney, whom I got along with the least. Then I forced on a polite smile. "I have to go chat with a few other people. I'm glad that you guys came."

I was irked about how they could treat Coral that way, and the way they said thanks for having fun with her was like they had set it up for me to do that from the beginning. That might have pissed me off more, now that I thought about it.

"Luna, have you seen Coral?"

"No, but I can look around for her."

"I've looked everywhere."

Luna grinned at me. "Did you look in your bed?"

"Funny," I retorted and grinned. "That might not be a bad place to look."

Luna laughed. "I'm sure she is around here someplace."

I kept looking, and a few minutes later, Silvia approached me. "I heard you were looking for Coral."

"Yes, have you seen her?"

"She left the party about an hour ago. She didn't look well and said she was going to bed. I completely forgot to tell you, but she said she was sorry for having to leave."

Sadness descended over me. "Oh, I'm sorry she's not feeling well. I was hoping to spend a little more time with her before I had to leave tomorrow morning."

"I didn't know you were leaving."

"I have a business trip that came up last minute."

"That's a shame. I'm so sorry, Landan. I know Coral would have stayed if she had been feeling better. She looked like she was going to throw up at any moment."

"Wow, that's horrible. I had no idea. I'll send her a message in a little while, and maybe I can sneak over to see her before it gets too late."

"I wanted to say happy birthday before I left. It was a wonderful party, and I told your mother how incredible your guesthouse is. Thank you all for your hospitality, Landan."

"My pleasure. I am glad that you enjoyed it, Silvia."

"And thank you for making Coral so happy. I haven't been in their lives very long, and this is the happiest I have seen Coral since I met her."

I took Silvia's hand. "Well, I hope I can make her a lot happier."

"I hope you can, too." She squeezed my hand and said good night.

After Silvia left, I spoke to a few more people, then sent Coral a message. *Hey, you. Silvia told me you weren't feeling well. I hope you are feeling better. I'd love to come over and see you for a few minutes if you're still awake.*

After sending the message, I slipped my phone back into my pocket and checked it about every five minutes to see if she replied, but by midnight, when the last guests were leaving, I still hadn't heard from her. Disappointed that I couldn't say goodbye to her, I hoped she would slip over to see me in the morning before I left. She knew that I was planning on leaving around four-thirty in the morning.

A few hours later, the first thing I did after I opened my eyes was grab my phone and see if she replied. There was nothing. Maybe she would surprise me.

I got dressed and went downstairs, looking out the window

toward the guesthouse, but no lights were on. Finally, I couldn't wait any longer, and I climbed in my car, pulled it out of the garage, and typed her a message, giving her final seconds to come running to me to say goodbye.

I am so sorry we didn't get to say goodbye. I hope you enjoy your last day, Coral. I'm going to miss you. I will be in touch soon.

I waited to see if there would be a reply, and when I couldn't wait a second longer, I drove down the driveway, glancing in the rearview mirror multiple times to see if she was running to catch me. What a romantic fool I was. My brothers would give me such grief.

I drove to the airport, recalling all the incredible moments I had shared with Coral over the last few days. As soon as this business deal was completed, I was going to find a way to see her and tell her we had to figure something out.

I parked at the airport and got through security about five minutes before my flight began to board. They were calling first class when my cellphone rang. Hoping it was Coral, I quickly pulled it out of my pocket, but it was Tim. I sent it to voicemail because I needed to board the plane.

Once seated, I checked my phone to see that Tim had left me a voicemail. I dialed in and listened to the message. "Hey, sorry to bother you, Landan, but I'm wondering if Coral is with you by any chance. Can you let us know if she is? Thanks."

Why would he think Coral is with me? I dialed his number, and he answered after the second ring. "Man, thanks for calling back so quickly. She decided to ditch us and go with you, right?"

"Ditch you? What are you talking about, Tim? Coral isn't with me. I haven't seen or spoken to her since last night at the party when she got sick."

"Well, shit!" He turned around and relayed the message to someone else. I heard someone speak, and Tim asked, "Are you at the airport now?"

"Yes, but I'm sitting on a plane, about to take off. Where is Coral?" Anxiety began to rush through me.

"We don't know. We got up this morning and found her bed empty. Silvia went in to check on her, and all her stuff is gone—"

"What do you mean her stuff is gone?" I asked.

"What?" he said, then told me to hold on. A moment later, he was back. "Alaina just checked her email and found that one of the rental cars was returned last night five minutes before midnight."

"None of you knew?"

"No, why would we be calling you if we did?" he retorted quickly.

Tension began to web through my veins. Where was she? Had she felt so bad that all she wanted to do was go home? Why would anyone who was sick wish to get on a plane? What the hell was going on? It was more like she was running away than she was feeling ill. Had someone said something to her at the party that upset her? Could something have upset her so much that she would run away?

"You better keep me updated. I'm getting ready to take off, but text me if you find her!"

"I will. Sorry for bothering you."

I didn't reply as I shook my head and put my phone on the armrest beside my seat. I stared out the window, wondering where she could have gone and why she had left.

The moment we could connect to the plane's Wi-Fi, I was connected and sent her a message. *Coral, where are you? I'm worried about you. What's going on?*

It was almost seven thirty when I received a text from Tim stating that Coral had gone home. She was currently in Minneapolis, waiting for a connecting flight.

I typed back a response. *Why did she leave?*

I don't know. Alaina pulled some strings and found out that she flew out on a red-eye from Reno to Vegas at one a.m., then took another flight to Minneapolis and will be landing in Harrisburg at about eleven.

Have you spoken to her?

No, her phone is off. She hasn't replied to anyone. Did something happen with you guys?

I have no clue what is going on, Tim. I am completely baffled.

Okay, if you hear from her, let me know, and vice versa.

You got it.

I fretted over what could have caused her to run away. Had she been frightened by how she felt? I didn't think that could be it. Had someone told her something about me that had upset her? I didn't think there was anything in my past that might have bothered her that much. She was the type of person to ask questions, not just run away. I had learned that much about her over the last few days.

I managed to get a few hours of sleep in between worrying about Coral and the business I had to attend to in Canada. At least we knew she was heading home. Why, I didn't know, but she was going home. If I had to fly back and forth across the continent, I would. I was going to get to her as soon as I could, and I was going to straighten this out. I cared too much about her not to do this.

I was about to go through customs in Canada when Tim sent me a text. *Can you talk?*

His message was ominous. *I just landed, what's up?*

I expected a text, but instead, he called. "Where are you?"

"Going through customs in Canada. Why? What's going on?"

He blew out a deep breath. "I don't know the details, and we are all getting packed right now to get back home, but we learned that Coral made it back there."

"And?" I said, stepping out of the line because I was next in line and didn't want to hang up.

"And, well, shit, she went to her café, and I don't know what the fuck is going on, but she got arrested there."

"She got arrested? What?" I spoke louder than I intended, and several customs officers looked at me with interest. "Why the fuck did she get arrested going to her own business?"

"I don't know. None of us do! Ethan called his department back home, but it's not local PD. It's federal."

"Federal?"

"Yes, the DEA picked her up and took her out of the café."

"How do you know this?"

"Because Coral called Ethan a few minutes ago, freaking out and demanding he find out what the hell is going on."

"What can I do?"

"Nothing right now, but I'll update you as soon as I find something out. How long are you in Canada?"

"At least two days here in Quebec, and then I have to go to British Columbia, but I am going to try and figure something out so I can get down there."

"Let us find out what is going on first, then you can figure out what you are going to do. What a fucking mess," Tim groaned.

"Keep me updated," I told him before we hung up.

Then I pulled out my passport and prepared to get grilled by the customs officers who were watching me as if they expected me to be carrying drugs on me.

CHAPTER TWENTY-ONE

CORAL

My mind was a mess. How could Landan pretend he cared about me like that when he was just spending time with me because my family asked him to? When had they? Whose idea was it? Candy? Evan? Riley? Maybe Carmen? It was probably Carmen, and she had Tim call Landan and get it all set up once she realized that Tim was friends with him. That had to be it.

Had Tim spoken to him that first night we arrived when he brought the welcome basket with his mother? Maybe Tim suggested it.

It didn't matter who came up with the stupid idea. I was furious with them all because I was pretty sure all of my siblings were in on it. A thought dawned on me—if my family was aware of it, was his? Did Luna pretend to be my friend because she knew what he was doing? How deep did this devastating betrayal go?

I didn't sleep at all on my first flight, but I managed to get a few hours on my second flight, and then I had to wait several hours for my third flight to take off, so I curled up on a bench and slept there.

It wasn't until I landed that I wondered what was happening at home. I hadn't spoken to Monica in days, although we had texted a few times. I had no clue if my business was still holding its own or was going under. At this moment, I hoped it was about to go belly up because I was ready to move on. I wanted to say goodbye to it all and walk away from Millerstown. Perhaps I would move to Texas to be near Cara. She was the only one who seemed to check in on me, and I knew she couldn't have been involved in this latest calamity. If I wasn't so upset about Landan, I could move to Lake Tahoe, but I would always be nervous to run into him.

Maybe I would look for another skiing town and move there. Wyoming, Colorado, and Montana all had some great slopes. I could find a job doing anything and spend my time off enjoying the freedom of skiing.

Walking down to collect my baggage, I turned on my phone. I knew I would have a slew of messages, and I was right. I ignored all the text messages because they were from family and Landan. I didn't want to hear their bullshit right now.

Just the thought of hearing Landan give some excuse for what he did made me want to curl up in a fetal position in the middle of the airport and cry.

There were no texts from Monica, and I was tempted not to listen to my messages, but I hadn't listened to them in days, and there might be some from suppliers. If I heard my siblings or Landan's voices, I would skip or delete the message. I would only listen to those messages that related to business.

I waited until I was downstairs near baggage claim, and then I stood in the corner and closed my eyes as the first message played. It was business, and I felt better as I listened to it. I saved it, then went on to the next one. It was a message from Candy when they were trying to find me after Dad fell. I skipped that one and then the next four. After that, it was another business message.

Then the messages from today began, and I skipped six from family members. The seventh message raised the hackles on my neck, and I froze.

It was Monica, but she was whispering hurriedly. "Coral, the police are here. They are arresting everyone. I don't know what is going on—" Her voice stopped, and I could hear someone in the background tell her to hang the phone up now.

I listened to the message three times, as if I expected to hear something else or that it would change or that there would be an explanation. Why were the police at my café? Why would they be arresting my employees? What the hell happened while I was away? My luggage was forgotten as I looked for signs for rental cars.

I began running and came to a skidded stop in front of one of the desks. "I need a car."

"Do you have a reservation?"

"No, but I need one now."

"I'm sorry, but all our cars are reserved. You can try one of the other rental agencies." Just like that, I was dismissed, and I growled and walked quickly to the next one and then the next one, only to be told the same thing. My luck changed at the last desk, and a few minutes later, she handed me a set of keys.

I ran out of the airport and located the car. Within moments, I was pulling out of the parking space and heading toward Millerstown. The last time I went on vacation, Chantel stole money from me. What had Monica done to get arrested?

I wanted to scream and pound my fists on the steering wheel. Why did I ever open a café? Why couldn't I have employees I could trust? Why couldn't I have people in place so I didn't have to do it all one hundred percent of the time?

I decided right then that I was going to sell the business. I was done with managing people and dealing with vendors, supplies, inventory, and customers. I could live cheaply and pack most of my precious possessions inside my car. I could go anywhere and work. I could move around, not even put down roots. I was finished with it all!

I drove as fast as I dared in the traffic on the highway and pulled into the parking lot of the strip mall where my café was located. I had tried to call Monica three times and each time it had gone to voicemail. I parked, staring at the front of my store and the closed sign hanging in the window. What the hell was going on? I dug through my purse to locate my keys, then jumped out and sprinted to the café door, shoving the key in as quickly as possible and disappearing inside. Two feet in, I froze.

My entire store was ransacked, like someone had broken in and trashed it. Suddenly, my heart dropped, and I ran into the back, slipping on coffee beans and grabbing the shelf to keep from falling on my ass. My eyes were wide as I took in the scene before me. Things were flipped over, cases emptied, and my latest shipment of Costa Rican coffee beans spilled all over the counter and floor.

I stared at it and cried out, "No! Oh, no, no, no!" I ran to them and began to collect the beans on the floor as I continued sobbing. "No!"

"Put your hands where we can see them!" a deep voice said from behind me.

I spun around, and two men stood with guns pointed at me. "I didn't do anything! Someone came in here and destroyed my café! I own this place!" I cried.

"You are confirming that you are Coral Winston?" one of the men said as he put his gun back into his holster and stepped forward.

"Yes, and this is my café."

He reached down and grabbed my wrist, none too gently. "Stand up, Ms. Winston. You're under arrest."

"What? What are you talking about? I don't know what is happening here. I was on vacation in Lake Tahoe with my family."

The cold, rigid cuffs clicked around my wrists, and I felt like I had been kicked in the gut. I couldn't breathe, think, or even speak as he yanked me unceremoniously toward the front of the café. Another man was standing off to the side, and I noted that on the upper left chest of his jacket, it said: DEA.

I was in shock as they dragged me out to the car, placed me against an SUV, patted me down, and then told me to get into it.

This was a bad dream. This was all a bad dream that started at Landan's birthday party. I must have had too much to drink, and I was having wild dreams. Was I drinking champagne? That had happened before. That was what this was. It couldn't be real.

However, the cold steel digging into my back sure felt real. Suddenly, my brain began to work again and with it my voice. "Why am I being arrested? Are you going to explain to me what is going on? I told you I was on vacation! I have no clue what is going on!"

"It will all be explained to you later."

"Do you know who I am?"

The man turned and glanced at me, smirking. "I hope so since we had a warrant for Coral Winston matching your description, and you confirmed that is who you are."

"Then you know my brother is a county detective," I stated, and he glanced at the man driving and chuckled.

"So? What does that have to do with your arrest?"

"I don't know what it has to do with my arrest because I don't even know why I am being arrested!" I shouted, ready to start flipping out if I didn't get answers.

"Relax, Ms. Winston. Everything will be explained to you later."

I glanced beside me. "My purse! My purse is in my car, and it's unlocked."

"I will have an agent collect it for you."

I leaned back against the seat as much as I could with my hands there. "When can I make a phone call?"

"You'll get your chance when we get to the office."

"Office? We aren't going to the police station?"

"Ma'am, we're the DEA, not cops. We work out of an office."

"Well, la-de-fucking-da! You work out of an office. I want to know what the hell is going on and call my brother." Ethan would be able to figure out what was going on, and he could get this all cleared up.

"You'd be much better off calling a lawyer," the guy said. And I huffed and stared out the window. I was so confused, and despite the stress, I was hungry and realized that I needed to pee.

"How did you know I was there?"

"Your passport was scanned, and we knew you were on your way home. We figured you would go to your house or your café, so we had people watching both locations."

"You were staking out my house and business?" I sighed. "I am not a criminal. I can't believe you are doing this to me."

"Save it for the judge," he stated, turning around to face forward. A few minutes later, we arrived, and they parked in the garage that was under the building and then brought me up to the fourth floor, where they took me down a hallway and opened a door into a small room.

I tensed and refused to step forward. "I have to use the restroom, and I want to make my phone call."

The guy looked annoyed and called for a woman to help me. I was mortified to have to use the bathroom with her watching me the entire time. She didn't even look away to give me privacy. Talk about feeling like a criminal, and I hadn't even done anything wrong.

When I was done, she let me wash my hands, then cuffed me in the front instead of behind my back, which was much better. Then she led me back to the small room and told me to have a seat. She released one wrist and attached that cuff to a large eye hook through the table.

I felt like I was in a nightmare. This had to be a bad dream. All those cop shows that I had seen in the past had accumulated in my mind and created this. I would never watch another cop show as long as I lived.

Finally, the man who arrested me returned to the room and sat down. In front of him was a file and he flipped it open.

"When can I call my brother?"

"Well, I figured you might want to know what the charges are."

"Of course I do. What crazy thing do you believe I did?"

"Well, the main charge for you is drug trafficking."

I stared at him. "Excuse me?"

"What did you not understand about that charge?"

"Why would you think I was doing anything with drugs? The only drugs I ever use are for headaches and allergies."

"Well, because we pulled two kilos of cocaine from your delivery of coffee beans." He gave me a smug look.

I stared at him, my mind going a million miles an hour. What the hell was he talking about? How could cocaine be in my coffee bean shipment? All those cop shows I had seen helped me decide on my next set of words. "I'd like to make my phone call now."

He gave me a crooked smile. "I thought you might."

CHAPTER TWENTY-TWO

CORAL

Two kilos of cocaine? How did two kilos of cocaine end up in my coffee beans? Who were they for?

The agent got up and left the room, saying he'd be back in a few minutes with a phone to make a call. I stared at the mirrored wall before me, wondering who was watching me on the other side. Was the agent watching to see if I would get nervous? I wasn't scared, I was pissed. I was furious that someone was screwing with me like this.

My family, Landan, and now my employees. I couldn't trust anyone. What did I do to deserve all this bad karma? I was always nice to people, and I would have given the shirt off my back to anyone who asked, and yet the universe appeared to be out to get me.

Almost thirty minutes later, the agent returned with a phone that he plugged into a jack on the wall. "You will have someone watching you, so you can't hurt yourself with the phone." He pointed at the mirror. "But the sound is off, and we won't be able to hear your conversation."

"Yeah, like I can trust you not to eavesdrop," I sneered. I had always respected anyone in law enforcement, but now that I had been arrested for no reason, I was starting to doubt them. Someone here hadn't done their investigation correctly.

What if I went to jail? What if someone framed me to make it look like I had done it? Panic began to claw through my gut as I picked up the phone and dialed Ethan's number. I knew all my family's cellphone numbers by heart, but his number was the most important one.

"Ethan Winston," he answered after the second ring.

"Ethan, it's Coral."

"Coral! Where the hell are you? Why did you leave? You left us in a bind, you know, taking one of the trucks."

"Shut up!" I screamed, near hysterics. "Ethan, just shut up, okay! I need your help. I'm in trouble, and I don't know what the hell is going on."

He grew instantly quiet and then asked, "Okay, what's up?"

I started to cry, the stress of all this causing my eyes to fill with moisture and spill over in an uncontrollable stream of salty tears. "I don't know what is happening, but I was arrested at my café."

"Arrested? What the fuck did you do, Coral?"

"I didn't do anything, Ethan!" I screamed at him and repeated, "I didn't do anything!" I began to sob.

"Coral, I need you to calm down. Who arrested you?"

"The DEA."

"Where did they arrest you? At the airport?"

"No, I was at the café. As soon as I arrived in town, I checked my message and had one from Monica saying the police were there. I went straight there and found my café tossed. Everything was a mess, and then the DEA came in behind me and pulled guns on me and arrested me! Like I'm a criminal!"

"What did you do?"

I sniffed. "What do you mean? What did I do? I already told you that I didn't do anything! Why would you assume I did something?"

"Did you do something that would cause them to think you broke the law, Coral? The DEA doesn't routinely poke their noses into cases that aren't big deals."

"I don't know what the hell is going on, Ethan! That's why I called you. I don't need you to give me a hard time. I need your help! They gave me one phone call, and I used it to call you! You need to find out what the hell is going on and get me out of this."

"Coral, I'm not sure what I can do. These guys are federal, not local or state. I don't have any pull with them."

I growled into the phone, "Well, you better find a way to help me! You and every single one of my siblings owe me this!"

He paused. "What are you talking about?"

I scoffed, "Like you don't know! Whatever, Ethan! Just find out what is going on."

"I'll contact a lawyer and have him come to you."

"Fine," I stated as the door opened beside me.

"Your time is up," the agent stated.

"I have to go, Ethan." I hung up before he could say anything else and pushed the phone toward the agent.

Before he left with the phone, he asked if I needed anything. "Yes, to get out of here because I'm innocent, but since I know that's *not* going to happen anytime soon, can I please have water or coffee, and something to eat, crackers, dry bread, whatever you feed innocent prisoners? I haven't eaten since yesterday."

How I could be hungry at this time was beyond me, but I was. Perhaps the shock of being arrested had depleted the last of my energy stores, and now I was running on fumes.

I sat there with my arms lying on the table and my head resting on my arms. I was exhausted, starving, confused, and angry all rolled into one. I wanted to scream, yell, and throw things, but I also wanted to curl up in the corner and cry like a baby.

Landan's image came to mind, and I shoved it away so hard

that I'd be surprised if it ever came back. Landan had no place in my mind right now. He had nothing to do with what was happening. But what was happening? I thought back on the message from Monica and the fear in her voice as she said the police were there, arresting everyone. Why did they arrest everyone at the café if they thought I was the one who was drug trafficking? Or did they think everyone had something to do with this?

I was contemplating which employee could have been responsible for this when the agent returned. A large bottle of water and a brown bag were in his hand. He set them on the table and then sat across from me.

"Hope you like ham and cheese." He pointed at the bag.

I'd eat liverwurst and onions right now if that was the best they could do. "Thank you, that will be fine." I opened the bag to find not only a sandwich on a Kaiser roll and not two plain slices of white bread, but a small bag of plain chips and an orange.

I set the items out, and even though I wanted to ravish them all, I made sure to eat slowly, as if I had all the time in the world. For all I knew, I did have all the time in the world before an attorney showed up here. An attorney—I never thought I would ever need one of those.

I took a bite of the sandwich, and even though it was dry, it was still good. After I chewed it, I studied the agent. "I don't remember if you ever told me your name."

"Agent Cruise," he responded.

I nodded and took another bite, chewing methodically as I wondered what else I could ask him. "Did you arrest everyone who was at the café?"

"We took all the employees working yesterday into custody. Most have been released."

"Most? Who is still in custody?"

"Monica Carson," he stated and observed me carefully.

Monica? Did she have something to do with this? I nodded and then went back to eating, putting all my attention on my food and ignoring him sitting there as I tried to picture Monica being involved in drugs. I had to admit that when I first met her, all the tattoos she had inked on her body kind of scared me, but she had a great personality and experience, so I let my first impression go. I had always been told not to judge a book by its cover. Cara's husband Bryan and Candy's fiancé Mike were prime examples of that.

I finished my sandwich and asked Agent Cruise if I could save my chips and orange for later. He told me he would put them aside for me and promptly left the room.

I toyed with the water bottle as I sat there thinking things over. I didn't have a watch on, as they had taken that and my phone. I had no idea how long I had been sitting here, but my back was killing me after traveling for so long and then sitting on this hard chair. I laid my head on my arms again and eventually dozed off.

I woke to the door opening and a man around forty stepping inside. He had dirty-blond hair cut short, intelligent brown eyes, and looked like he could have played football in his younger days with the width of his shoulders. "Coral Winston, I'm Thad Montgomery. I'm going to be your attorney."

Whew! Finally, someone on my side. "Hello, Mr. Montgomery."

"Call me, Thad, please."

I nodded as he took a seat across from me. "Are you physically all right? Have they let you use the restroom? Have they given you anything to eat? Has anyone acted in an unprofessional manner?"

I shook my head at the barrage of questions. My mind was still foggy from sleep. "No, they have been all business and professional. I used the restroom when I got here, and they gave me a sandwich, but I didn't eat the chips or orange that came with it."

He nodded. "Okay, that's good that they have treated you fairly." He pulled out a notepad, a pen, and a small stack of papers. He turned the documents toward me. "Have they told you what they are charging you with?"

"No." I shook my head. "Not really. Agent Cruise only said I was being charged with drug trafficking because they found two kilos of cocaine in my coffee beans."

"How did those drugs get in the coffee beans?"

I shrugged. "I have no idea, Thad. I have never used drugs in my life, and there is no way in hell I would ever sell them!"

He studied me, and I knew he was trying to see if he could trust me. "I know people say I swear to God that I'm innocent when they aren't, but I have no reason to lie. I do not know how the drugs got there, and if I did, I would tell them everything I knew."

"Tell me the process of where the beans come from."

I went on to explain how I sourced the beans after doing a lot of research, and then I purchased the beans in large quantities to be shipped to me monthly so I could roast them before using them. I explained it all, from how they were sent to how they went through customs and how they were delivered. I have received a shipment a month for the last six years and never had a problem until now.

"What about Monica?"

"What about her?"

"I understand she is still being questioned, but I also believe that she has stated that you knew that the drugs were coming in through the coffee beans."

"*What?*" The two of us stared at each other. "Monica said I knew?"

"She did."

I sat straight up in my chair, my hands splayed on the table.

"That is a bald-faced lie! How dare she accuse me of something like this!"

"How well do you know Monica?"

"I don't know. I mean, we talk, but we don't really talk. She's not a close friend. She's an employee. Her criminal record was clean, and her credit score was good."

"You do a credit check on your employees?"

I nodded. "Yes, I do. After a previous assistant manager stole from me because she had a lot of debt, I started doing credit checks to make sure I wasn't hiring someone in dire need of funds. I learned my lesson with that one."

"Okay, I'll see what I can find out about her. Maybe I can find something that they haven't found. If she is saying you knew, then chances are that she's the one who is involved."

I put my hands over my face and rubbed at my weary eyes. "What happens now?"

"Well, they are going to do a bail hearing, and hopefully, we can get you out on bail."

"How much do you think that will be?"

"For this large of a quantity, and the fact that you do have access to private planes and unlimited funds—"

"But I don't. I barely have the money to pay my mortgage and car payment."

"Do you think that they don't know who your sister-in-law is?"

I sighed. "I'm sure they do."

"How did you find out about this?"

"I was on my way home, and when I got to the airport, I was listening to my messages. Monica left a message and stated that the police were there and arrested everyone. I raced to the café to find out what was happening and walked into a huge mess. My café was destroyed. Everything was torn apart."

"They were probably searching to see if you had anything else illegal there."

"I don't have anything illegal there! Those drugs shouldn't have been either! But somehow, they showed up there—and when I was out of town! Isn't that a coincidence?"

"Well, I will do some searching and see what else I can find. For now, I need you to sit tight. I think you are being arraigned at ten o'clock tomorrow morning."

"Tomorrow? Do you mean I have to stay here overnight?"

"Unfortunately, Coral, they will put you in a holding cell after they talk to us in a few minutes. They only have arraignment for a few hours on Sunday. Be glad they aren't holding you over until Monday. They are going to want to ask you a lot of questions. If you are innocent, then there is nothing to hide. Be honest, but if I tell you to refrain from answering, no matter your answer, then refrain. Do you understand?"

"Yes, I understand," I told him, but what I really was understanding was that I was going to be spending the night in jail. I wanted to vomit.

CHAPTER TWENTY-THREE

LANDAN

It took me longer than usual to get through customs, but eventually, I did. The fact that I was overly anxious to find out what was going on didn't help me deal with them.

When I was on the other side, I called Tim back. "Have you learned anything?"

"No, not yet, but I'm going to let you talk to Ethan. He knows more about what is going on. We are on the way to the airport now."

"Fine, put him on."

"Hey, Landan."

"What do you know, Ethan?"

"All I could find out was that the DEA seized two kilos of cocaine from a shipment of coffee beans at her café. They had an arrest warrant ready for her when she arrived back in town, and they were waiting for her at the café when she went there."

"Who is setting your sister up?"

"I don't know. For all I know, Coral could have shipped the drugs in herself."

"Come on, Ethan! You can't believe your sister would do

something like that! I barely know her, and I know she's not capable of that type of behavior."

"You might think you know her, Landan, but you don't know her that well. She has cut herself off from us over the last year. None of us know what is going on with her."

I ground my teeth, wanting to lash out, but I needed to keep my cool, or I'd get shut out. "Have you hired her an attorney yet?"

"No, I was just trying to come up with one I might know."

"Forget it, I have a guy. I'll deal with the attorney."

"Landan, Coral is not your responsibility."

"She might not be, but I don't think she is guilty. You obviously aren't sure. Besides, I can afford to hire the best, can you?"

"Hey, man, you do whatever you want," he said with irritation in his voice.

"Don't worry, I will."

I hung up without another word and stalked toward the baggage claim, searching my phone for a contact number. I was on the escalator going down when I hit call, and it was answered on the third ring.

"Landan Lancaster, as I live and breathe. How the hell are you doing?"

"Hey, Thad. I've been better. I need your help."

"Personally or professionally?"

"A little of both."

"Are you in trouble?"

"No, it's not me, it's a—" I paused, unsure what to call her. "It's someone very important to me." I was at the bottom of the escalator and glanced over the signs held by the drivers waiting for their passengers. I waved at one of the men when I saw my name, and he began to follow me as I went toward the baggage claim.

"All right, tell me what you know and what you want me to do."

"I want you to find out where the DEA office is near Miller-stown, Pennsylvania. They arrested a woman named Coral Winston, who lives in that town and runs a coffee shop. They are charging her with drug trafficking. From what I understand, they found two kilos of coke in a delivery of coffee beans that she gets from her supplier in Costa Rica."

"Is she guilty?"

"I would stake my life on the fact that she is not, Thad. This woman doesn't have a criminal bone in her body."

"Okay, what did you say her name is?"

I gave him the information again and told him that I would get there as soon as possible, but I was in Canada and needed to oversee a critical business deal.

He told me he would keep me updated and ended the call just as my suitcase came down the chute. I picked it up, and the driver of my car took it from me as he asked if there was more. After telling him no, I followed him to the vehicle, wishing I could head back to the ticket agent and book a flight to Penn-sylvania.

I WAS on pins and needles for the next few hours. I met with my client and turned over the paperwork. He said he would get back to me early the following day, and I booked my next flight to British Columbia for later in the day. If all went well, I could be on another flight back to the States and Pennsylvania by Monday night.

Thad called me later that night. "How is she?"

He chuckled. "I can see why you like her. She's a firecracker. She's upset, confused, and tired, but she's okay. She's a fighter."

I released a pent-up breath as my eyes closed. "I'm glad she's okay. They aren't being assholes, are they?"

"No, they are treating her as well as they can."

"Is she out on bail?"

"Her bail hearing is tomorrow morning. She's in their lockup for the night, not in a county jail."

"Thank God, whatever her bail is set at, I will pay it. I don't care how much it is."

"I figured as much. She's pretty adamant about being set up."

"Do you believe her?" That was the first time I wondered if I was blind to the fact that she might be guilty. Ethan was right; I didn't know her well, but I believed that she was good in my heart.

"Yes, I do. She seems like a great person, and she is being very honest. I am looking into the other people who work at the café. They were still holding the assistant manager, and she said that Coral was aware of the drugs."

"That bitch."

"I have a feeling it's going to be the assistant manager to blame for this, not Coral, but I need to do some digging. I'm going to hire a private investigator to look into her. Do you have a problem with that?"

"You can hire a dozen of them. Whatever you need, Thad. I appreciate you doing this."

"You're welcome. She's resting for now. I waited to make sure she was in her cell before I left. I will be there for the arraignment tomorrow and let you know what happens."

"Thank you, Thad." I paused. "Did you tell her that I hired you?"

"No, I didn't. It didn't come up, and I wasn't sure if you would want me to say anything. I know her sister-in-law is very wealthy. She probably assumes that she is paying for my services. Do you want me to tell her?"

Did I? No, I guess I didn't. I still wasn't sure what had happened on Friday night and why she left so suddenly without saying anything. "No, that's okay. Let her keep thinking that it's her sister-in-law. I am sure she will find out soon enough."

"You got it. I hope you can get some rest."

"Thanks, Thad, and I can't thank you enough."

"My pleasure, but next time you call me, it better be because you are in town and want to go cut for a beer and a game of pool."

"You got yourself a deal, Thad. Have a good night."

"Night, Landan."

After I hung up with him, I called Luna to let her know what was going on. She told me that she was at the airport getting ready to take a red-eye to Pennsylvania and would keep me updated on anything that happened once she got there.

"Luna, you know you don't have to do that."

"Landan, of course I do. I can tell how much she means to you, and I bet it is tearing you up inside not to be there for her right now. I know you have things you have to do. I want her to know she's not alone and you are worried about her."

I breathed a sigh of relief. "I appreciate you more than you know, Luna. I really do."

"I know you would do the same for me."

"I would, without question." I paused. "What bugs me is that her family should be doing it too."

"They did fly home right away," she replied.

"Yeah, but when I spoke to her brother, Ethan, he questioned if she was innocent."

"Are you serious? There is no way that Coral would be trafficking drugs! I barely know the woman, but she's not the type of person to do that."

"I know, but it makes me wonder if maybe she is involved, and I don't know her as well as I thought."

"Landan, you have always trusted your gut instinct on people. Our whole family does, and none of us could see her being a criminal mastermind."

I chuckled. "Yeah, I know. I guess I just don't know what to think, and I'm feeling off because I can't get there to talk to her. It doesn't help matters that I don't even know why she left."

"No one seems to understand that, but we will figure it out when there is time. You try to get some rest to take care of business, but I will keep you updated. They are calling for my flight to board, so I need to go."

"Safe travels, and I love you, Luna."

"I love you too, Landan. I'll talk to you later."

After I hung up with Luna, I called my mother to let her know about the business deal so she could relay that to my father when she spoke with him and advise her on what was going on with Coral.

Like Luna, she was one hundred percent on Coral's side, and I hung up feeling a bit better. When I lay down to try and sleep, all I could think about was how Coral was locked up in a cell someplace, alone and scared.

I was in the same time zone as Coral was, and my anxiety was through the roof as I waited for word from someone. Thad had messaged me saying that he found some information on the assistant manager that might help Coral's case and would speak to me about it later once they had the arraignment.

Luna was there but couldn't see her, but she would be present in the courtroom and try to speak to her then.

All I could do was wait and deal with the business at hand. I was pacing my hotel room, staring out the window at the city below, and wishing like hell that I was in Pennsylvania.

Every time my phone made a notification, I'd jump to see what it was, but it took forever to finally hear something.

Luna called me, and I didn't bother with pleasantries when I answered. "What is going on?"

"Her bail was set for one million, and she had to surrender

her passport. They wanted to put her on house arrest, but Thad talked them out of that as she has no criminal past and no proof that she is guilty here."

"One million? Jesus, they aren't playing games, are they?"

"My understanding is that the judge's son died from a cocaine overdose, and he takes drug cases very seriously. That's why they pushed for her to be arraigned today and not last night."

"Pricks," I muttered.

"Exactly, but the money is already being transferred. I took care of that for you." She hesitated, and I could tell she wanted to say more. "She wouldn't talk to me, though, Landan."

"She wouldn't? Did she say anything?"

"No, she saw me and looked shocked at my presence and then glanced around the room, probably to see if you were there, but then she turned her back to me and told Thad that she didn't want to speak to me."

"Why the hell would she do that?"

"Maybe because she is mortified about this."

"Possibly," I replied. "Were her siblings there?"

"Silvia and her father were there, Ethan too, but no one else."

"Did she talk to them?"

"She spoke to her father, but when her brother approached her, she refused to speak to him. I think her father and Silvia are going to take her home."

"Okay, I appreciate all you have done, Luna."

"How are things going there?"

"Too fucking slow!" I growled. "I should hear from them soon, and then I will head out immediately to jump on a flight."

"Do you want me to stay here? Maybe I can talk to her once she gets home."

"No, I appreciate it, but if she is feeling embarrassed by this, I need to be the one to tell her not to be."

"Okay, then I might stick around and check the place out. Let me know if you change your mind."

"I will, and thank you again, Luna. I appreciate you taking care of the bail for me."

"Don't mention it, Landan. Love you!"

"Love you too."

After we hung up, I stared out the window. Coral was being released on one million dollars bail. At least she was being released. I couldn't get this business deal over with fast enough.

CHAPTER TWENTY-FOUR

CORAL

T had and Agent Cruise returned a little while later, and I was prepared to tell them everything I knew. I had nothing to hide.

"Why were you in Lake Tahoe?" Agent Cruise started off by asking.

"I was on vacation with my family. It was my birthday present, and they all decided to go."

"If it was your present, why did they all go?"

I laughed. "Because I never take time off, and they knew that if they didn't force me to, I wouldn't go."

"Why don't you take time off?"

"Because my café is important to me. It's all I have."

"Is money an issue?" he asked.

I frowned. "Isn't money an issue for everyone?"

"I'm asking the questions, Ms. Winston."

I sighed. "Money is always an issue when you own a small business. The landlord keeps upping my lease payment, and the cost of other supplies is always rising, too."

"How much do you make a month?"

I blinked. "I don't know."

"Don't you pay yourself a salary?"

"I do, but it's not that much."

"Then how much do you pay yourself?"

"I don't know, I think it's like twenty-five hundred a month. Enough to pay for my mortgage, car payment, and utilities."

"How much do you have in your savings account?"

A burst of laughter flew out of my mouth. "Savings? I just told you I make twenty-five hundred a month. How much do you think I have in savings after paying my monthly bills?"

He looked pointedly toward me, and Thad touched my arm. "Coral, do you know how much you have in savings?"

"Not off the top of my head. If you give me my phone, I can look it up."

Agent Cruise pulled out a piece of paper. "Coral, is this your bank account number?" He read off a series of digits.

"Yes, it is." I had memorized it many years ago. I was still using the same checking and savings account I had as a teenager.

He flipped the paper around to me and tapped a finger on it. "Can you please tell me what the balance is?"

I glanced at the bottom, and my jaw dropped. "That's not my account."

"You just said it was."

"First off, how do you have my account information? And second, that is not my account! I have never had two hundred thousand dollars deposited into my account—ever!"

"Well, you do now. Care to explain how you got that?"

I glanced at Thad. He was sitting quietly like he was interested in the answer, too. "I have no clue! Can't you trace the deposit? If you could get into my account without my permission, you could trace the money back to who gave it to me."

"We did trace it. It came back to an account in Costa Rica."

I blinked and then blinked again. "I have a question for you, Agent Cruise. If I was purchasing drugs from a supplier in

Costa Rica, wouldn't I be sending them money, not the other way around?"

"Perhaps you are selling it for them, and that is your payment."

"No."

"No?"

"No, absolutely no! I told you that I am not selling drugs. I have never in my life used drugs, nor have I ever purchased anything that was not from a pharmacy. That cocaine is *not* mine!"

"Then whose is it?"

"That's your job to figure out," I stated as I sat back and crossed my arms. "Don't you think it's weird that it arrived at my café while I was out of town?"

"My understanding is that it was late to arrive. You expected it to be delivered a few days before you went on vacation."

"Yes, that's true."

"Then it arrived, but you weren't there to remove the drugs and give them to your dealer."

"Dealer? I don't have a dealer!"

"So you sell it yourself? Is it something anyone can purchase off your menu? Or only for select clientele?"

"You're not listening to me! I do not sell it! I have never even seen cocaine before, much less two kilos of it! Aren't you looking into other possibilities? What about Monica?"

"What about Monica?"

"What does she have to say?"

"She told us that you gave explicit instructions not to touch the delivery of beans until you got back. She said you never allow them to accept the shipment and that you tend to it yourself when no one else is around."

My God! That woman was trying to frame me in this. "Yes, I tend to my shipment because I have not taught anyone else how to check the beans or roast them."

185

"Because you want to get the drugs out first, right?"

"No! I don't deal drugs! I have never received a shipment of drugs before in my life. If I had ever opened one of my packages and found drugs, I would have been the first to call the police." Then I thought for a moment. "Wait!" I leaned up to the table as Agent Cruise raised a brow. "Last month, one of my boxes had been opened but resealed. I figured it was customs checking to ensure it contained what I stated. Maybe someone else got into it before I did and removed drugs then."

"Are you saying that you received a shipment of drugs previously?"

"No, I am not saying that. I am saying that I just remembered that the box from last month had been opened. Is it impossible that the person selling the drugs went into the box first? What if that is a possibility?"

"You just conveniently remembered that?"

"I didn't have a reason to think about it before, and it's not like I am well rested and on the top of my game here. Yes, I just remembered it."

"Do you have any proof?"

I thought about that for a moment. Did I still have the box? I sat up straighter, excited for the first time. "I think I do. The box was banged up, so I took a picture in case I needed to put a claim in. The pictures are on my phone. I don't think I deleted them; the box is still in my office. I used it for paperwork that I was going to put into storage. I distinctly remember that the tape was different than the original packing tape; that's what caught my eye in the first place, and I knew it had been previously opened."

He stared at me as if wondering if he should believe me. "I permit you, and I will do so in writing, so you don't need to get a warrant, to go back to my café and collect the box beside my desk. Just let me have my phone for a moment, and I will show you the pictures of the box."

He tapped his fingers on the table and then got up and disappeared from the room.

I turned to Thad. "Was that good? Is that good information?"

"Yes, that is good information, Coral. Good thinking. I'm glad you remembered it."

A few minutes later, the agent returned. "Sorry, but your phone has already been sent to forensics to be cloned and checked."

"You're cloning my phone? Why?"

"To check for your illegal business doings," he stated.

"I'm not doing anything illegal!" I hissed, and Thad put his hand on my forearm. I forced myself to calm down before I spoke again. "What about the box? Are you going to go check that?"

"We will look into it." He collected his papers. "For now, we are taking you to a cell for the night, and you will remain there until your arraignment tomorrow."

"But if you go get the box right now, you will see I am telling you the truth! Then you can drop the charges."

"Sorry, can't do that, Ms. Winston. An agent will escort you to your holding cell, and I will see you tomorrow in court." He nodded at Thad, and then he disappeared from the room.

"They aren't even going to check into my story?" I asked Thad as tears began to fill my eyes again. I hadn't cried this much in one day since my mother had passed.

"I will make sure they look into it, Coral. I swear, I will make sure they do. Before they come back, tell me everything you know about Monica."

I filled him in on anything I could remember about her, and we were just finishing up when a female agent opened the door.

"I know it's not going to be easy, but try to get some rest, and I will see you in the morning. I am going to my hotel and I will start looking into this information."

"Thank you so much, Thad." He squeezed my arm as we

couldn't shake hands since mine were still attached to the eye hook on the table.

As Thad stepped out, the female traded places with him and unlocked the cuffs. She walked me down several hallways, and then we were buzzed in through a door. It was cooler back here, and I could hear someone shouting down the hallway.

"I need to search you again before you can go into the cell."

I turned around and put my hands up in the air. "Go ahead."

"No, I am going to remove your cuffs, and you will have to strip all your clothes off and put on these sweatpants, sweatshirt, and socks."

"You are strip-searching me?"

She nodded, and I felt my last shred of dignity deflate as she unlocked my cuffs.

I DIDN'T SLEEP. I barely closed my eyes. I was exhausted the next morning and ready for this to end. They let me dress back in my clothes from the day before and gave me a breakfast burrito with a lukewarm cup of coffee. I finger-combed my hair and waited.

Finally, two agents came to get me and escorted me to an SUV that took me to the courthouse. As I sat there, I wondered how many of my siblings would be coming, and if any of them had told Landan what had happened. Not that Landan would care. He probably heard the news and was glad that I was gone.

When I stepped into the courtroom, my knees shook, and my hands were cuffed and secured to my waist with a thick leather belt. I was ashamed of myself, and I hadn't even done anything.

I saw my father first and Silvia sitting beside him. My father was stoic, but Silvia tried to smile through her watery gaze to let me know she was there for me. Beside my father was Ethan, and I glared at him before skimming the rest of the people present.

I almost stumbled when I saw Luna. What was she doing here? Was she here so she could report to Landan? Maybe they were worried it would somehow tarnish their name. It didn't matter why she was there. I had nothing to say to her. I was too mortified at being seen like this. The last thing I wanted was for her or her family to see me this way.

As I sat down, I made sure to tell Thad that I didn't want to talk to anyone but my father and Silvia. He glanced at me. "You don't want to talk to Luna?"

I blinked, surprised that she had introduced herself to my attorney. "No, I have nothing to say to her."

"Are you sure?"

"Yes," I replied and kept my face straight. She could report all this to her brother later; he would be glad I was out of his life for good. So much for ever going back to Lake Tahoe.

CHAPTER TWENTY-FIVE

LANDAN

I was in British Columbia now, and the clients took forever to sign off on the project. I had expected them to take a day or two at the most, but it had been three days.

Thad had kept me updated, and I knew Coral was home now. Her café was closed for the unforeseeable future. I had tried to contact her multiple times, but at first, her phone went to voicemail, and now it said that her number was disconnected.

I was utterly confused about what had happened between us. Things had been going great, better than I could have ever expected. I saw a future with her, one that was even better than I visualize with Eve or anybody else before that. I wanted to marry her, grow old with her, adopt babies we could raise together, and enjoy every moment we could.

I even pictured taking her with me on business trips around the world. I'd help her fill up her passport and treat her better than anyone had ever treated her.

It had now been six days since I had seen, spoken to, or looked into her beautiful blue eyes. I knew she was going through something horrible, but she could trust me. I wanted her to trust me and allow me to be there for her. Why wasn't she letting me?

My phone rang, and I glanced at the screen, then quickly grabbed it. "Hello?"

"Mr. Lancaster, it's Ira. We have the documents ready for you."

I closed my eyes. "Are they signed?"

"Yes, sir, they are."

Thank God! "Okay, I will pick them up in an hour."

"I'm sorry, sir, but Mr. Lambert has them at home and would like you to join him for dinner tonight."

The last thing I wanted to do was socialize with Mr. Lambert, but I couldn't say no. My father had taught me better than that. "Very well, let me know the address and the time."

"Mr. Lambert has a car scheduled to pick you up at five-thirty."

"Five-thirty it is, thank you."

The minute I was off the phone with Ira, I called my mother so she could relay the message to my father. "You will be home tomorrow then?" she asked.

"No, I'm going to fly straight to Pennsylvania."

"Landan, I don't think you should do that for two reasons."

"What are those two reasons, Mom?"

"First, those documents are too important not to deliver in person. Your father will expect them on his desk when he returns on Saturday night."

That was true, but I wanted to know the second reason because I felt that one was more personal. "And the other reason?"

"Have you spoken to her?"

"No, that's why I want to go see her."

"If she wouldn't talk to Luna, what makes you think she will talk to you?"

"Mom, I will make her talk to me. I know she wouldn't talk to Luna only because she was embarrassed."

"She might well be, but if she doesn't want to talk to you, do you think you should force it, Landan?"

"Yes, Mom, I do."

"Does she mean that much to you?"

"Mom, she means more to me than anyone I have ever met. She might be embarrassed to see me or even be mad that I came, but she is going to know that I would have been there the entire time if I could have been. I want her to know what she means to me."

"Can't you just call her?"

"She wasn't taking my calls, and it seems she changed her phone number now."

"Landan, that should tell you something."

"Sorry, I'm not trying to read between the lines here, Mom. If what I thought we had isn't real, or if she doesn't want to have anything to do with me, then she can say it to my face. I deserve at least that much."

"That is true." She sighed. "You do deserve an explanation."

"Thanks for understanding, Mom. I will catch a flight back tomorrow. Mr. Lambert wants to have dinner with me tonight, and then after I drop off the documents to you, I will fly out to Pennsylvania to see Coral."

"Okay, Landan. How about I meet you at the airport? Then you can pass them on to me and take off."

"That would be great, but I need to get home and repack my suitcase. I don't see myself needing a bunch of suits in Pennsylvania, plus I have a couple things I need to do before I head back out."

"That's probably a good idea anyway. Let me know when you are going to be in town."

"I will, bye, Mom," I told her and hung up, glancing at my

watch to see that I needed to get dressed so I wouldn't make the car wait long.

I COULDN'T SLEEP, so I was on my computer and decided to search on Coral. The search found several recent newspaper articles discussing the arrest and charges filed against her.

Thad had told me that she had given them information that could have helped clear her name, but he wasn't sure if they were looking into it yet. After the arraignment, he had to head back to Philadelphia, where his office was. I almost asked him for Coral's number but decided that it was probably better that I didn't. I wanted to talk to her face-to-face.

I skipped over the most recent articles after reading two and then found a link to Coral's Coffee Café. I clicked on the link and frowned. There was a notice on the first page of the website that said the business was currently closed until further notice. Was that her doing? Or was that the DEA that had closed her down?

I searched a little more and found a few social media accounts, but they were all private, and I didn't think she would accept a friend request if I sent one, so I didn't.

I finally drifted off to sleep a little later and dreamed of skiing down one of the slopes on Kirkwood with her. Her hair flew behind her, and she'd look over her shoulder at me and grin as I tried to keep up. God, I wanted to catch her and never let her go, but suddenly, we were going through trees, and she was getting too far ahead. I couldn't keep up with her and lost track of her. When I finally exited the trees, she was nowhere to be seen. I looked everywhere, but she had vanished. There weren't even any tracks in the snow. Maybe she had come out a different way, but all the paths led here, and as I waited, I realized that I was too late. Coral was already gone. The woman I wanted in my life more than anything had vanished practically before my eyes and I didn't understand how it could have happened.

I woke with a start and lay there staring at the ceiling while my heart hammered in my chest. Please don't let it be too late, I prayed as I continued to stare at the shadowed ceiling.

———

THE FOLLOWING DAY, I flew back to Lake Tahoe. Ten hours later, I was having dinner with my mother at my parents' house. My father was due the next night. Mom wanted me to stay at her house that night, but I wanted to go home, repack my suitcase, and sleep in my bed for at least one night.

When I stepped into my house, it felt odd. It was quieter than it should have been, and I stood at the back window for a long time, staring out over the lake. My heart ached with how much I missed Coral, and I knew that tomorrow, I might find out that she never wanted to speak to me again. If I thought recovering from the breakup with Eve was difficult, I was kidding myself because not having Coral in my life would tear me apart.

I showered and repacked my suitcase. Then I lay in bed, staring at the pillow on the other side and picturing her laughing as she lay there. I let the imaginary sound fill my ears and warm my soul. For the first time since my birthday party, I fell asleep and slept the entire night in peace.

———

SATURDAY MORNING, I was at the Reno airport as the sun rose. I was anxious to get going and knew it would be a very long day.

I had ten hours of travel time, and with as many time zones as I had traveled through this week, you would think my body would be a mess. However, I was fresh and ready to see her. Somehow, sleeping in my bed, where I had been with her, had helped to soothe the worry and allowed me to rest properly.

As I traveled, I answered emails and worked on a few things that needed my attention. It had been over a week since I had been in my office, but luckily, I had a great assistant who kept me in the loop and could take care of many things without bothering me.

It took me fourteen hours to finally arrive in Harrisburg, Pennsylvania, due to the weather in the area. I collected my rental SUV, but instead of finding her immediately, I decided to head to my hotel. It was late, and I didn't want to bang on her door in the middle of the night. Thad had been nice enough to supply me with her address and that of the café.

As I drove to the hotel, the windshield wipers whipped back and forth to remove the heavy flakes as they landed. It had stopped snowing long enough for us to land, but barely. The snow was coming down heavily again, and I was driving slowly. I didn't know these roads, so I took my time.

Once at my hotel, I collapsed into bed and fell sound asleep. I knew I would need to be wide awake and ready to plead my case with Coral tomorrow.

I was up a bit later than I had intended, but it was Sunday, and I figured she wouldn't be doing much today.

I ate breakfast at the hotel and then searched for her house. When I found it, I sat in the driveway for a few seconds and studied the humble dwelling. It was a small ranch house, but it looked well maintained. There was no garage, and it was obvious that a car had been parked there because of the void in the snow, but the tire marks suggested it had recently left.

I would check the café, and if she wasn't there, I would come back here and wait. She would return sooner or later.

I pulled into the strip mall parking lot where her café was located. It was dark inside, and most businesses around it were also dark. There were two cars parked in front of the café, and as I parked, a man stepped out of the door, holding a box.

I jumped out of my vehicle and rushed toward the door to catch it before it closed in case it automatically locked. "Hey, can you hold that?" I called out as the man began to step away from the door.

He looked at me, his gaze drifting down my torso and back up. "The business is closed," he stated gruffly.

"I know. I'm a friend of the owner."

"You're a friend of Ms. Winston?"

"Yes, who are you?" I asked, feeling as if I should be wary of this man.

"Agent Cruise, DEA."

I nodded and ground my teeth so I didn't lash out at him about having the wrong person.

"And you are?"

"Landan Lancaster."

His brows popped. "Well, Mr. Lancaster, she's in the back office. Have a nice visit." He walked away, and I grabbed the door right before it closed.

I stepped in, glancing around at the disarray inside. Obviously, she hadn't been able to start cleaning up. I wondered if she was allowed to now.

I heard a noise in the back and slipped around the counter. There were cups and coffee beans spilled everywhere, and I stepped carefully to avoid falling. I stepped through the door to the back and froze.

Coral sat on her knees, scooping coffee beans with her bare

hands. She sniffed, and I knew she was crying without seeing her face. My heart ached to go to her, but I couldn't do that until I knew why she had left.

"Coral?" I called softly, and she froze with her hands in midair. Her palms opened, and the beans spilled back to the ground as her face turned in slow motion toward me.

26

CHAPTER TWENTY-SIX

CORAL

It had all been a bad dream. Going through the arraignment, then having a one-million-dollar bail set. I would have been stuck in jail if it weren't for Alaina and Evan. No one else in my family had that kind of money.

I had spent most of my time at home, thinking over what would happen to me if I went to jail. I had nightmares about it and prayed several times a day that they would get it all figured out before my trial in three months. I had three months of freedom, and with the evidence they had against me—all fabricated to make me look guilty—there was no doubt I would be found guilty.

When I wasn't stressing over my future, I was trying not to think about Landan. That might have been worse than thinking about jail, but then I was grateful that at least I got almost a week of fun before my life turned to hell again. I wondered what he thought of me now.

After my phone continued to ring incessantly with reporters and people threatening me, I closed my account. I opened a new one with a different number I had only given to my father, Silvia, and Cara. Cara was the only one of my siblings I would talk to. I had even changed the locks on my doors so Carmen and Candy couldn't let themselves in. After a few days, they all seemed to leave me alone.

It was better that way. At least, that was what I told myself.

Today was the first day I was allowed to return to my café. Agent Cruise was finally going to take custody of the box I had told him about, and hopefully, it would help them realize that I was telling the truth.

Seeing the state of my café almost brought me to my knees again when I stepped inside with him. I unconsciously swiped a tear from my cheek as I showed him where the box was. He had finally been convinced to investigate the box after my phone was forensically analyzed and they saw that there were indeed pictures of a box with dents and tears in it and that it had a different kind of tape over the original shipping tape. They also recovered the email where I reported the damage to the shipping company.

"Did you guys have to tear this place apart like you did?" I asked him softly as I flipped the light on in my office.

"Sorry, just making sure we checked every place thoroughly."

I scoffed and shook my head. They could have been nicer about it. I could not imagine doing this to someone, and I wondered if Ethan did this during his search warrants.

"Here it is, right where I told you it would be."

He snapped pictures of it with his phone. "Can you remove the papers inside of it?"

"Yes," I told him and piled the papers on my desk while he put gloves on his hands.

When I was done, I stepped back, and he took a few more pictures before picking it up and inspecting each side and then the tape. "I'm going to take this for evidence."

"Go ahead. It only supports my defense that I had nothing to do with this."

"Maybe, but maybe not."

I didn't care anymore. I had resigned myself to the possibility that I would be going to jail. "Now, if you need nothing else, you can show yourself out."

"Have a good day, Ms. Winston."

"Yeah, whatever," I muttered, turning my back on him. He was cocky, and I didn't care for him. Maybe the fact that he had held me at gunpoint also had something to do with that.

I stood in my small kitchen/storeroom and took in the mess. I thought I heard someone talking out front, but the agent was probably harassing someone else. The less I saw of him, the better.

I sank to my knees and began to pull the beans toward me into a pile near my legs, and the waterworks started again. I wasn't sure what I was crying for now. I seemed to be blubbering constantly. If I thought there was any possibility that I could be pregnant, I would have taken a test, but I knew there was no chance.

"Coral?" A deep voice like the one I heard echo in my head when I thought of Landan came from behind me, and I froze. No. He couldn't be here! I was imagining it. I slowly turned and saw him standing only five feet away.

I stared at him, wanting to jump up and throw myself into his arms, but there was no reason to. He had used me, and I had no idea why the hell he would be here. "We are closed for good. Please leave," I stated and turned around, pushing myself off the hard tile floor and dusting my hands off on my jeans.

"Coral, we need to talk."

I glanced at him, feeling weak in the knees at how handsome he looked. I, on the other hand, looked like a train wreck. "We have nothing to say to one another."

"How can you say that?"

I laughed loudly. "How can I not? You had your fun, and there is no reason for you to be here other than to wallow in my shame. You've seen me at my worst now. You can go."

I went to step away, but Landan had a longer stride and grabbed my arm. "I am not leaving until we talk."

"There is nothing to say, Landan. I know why you did it. I'll get over it eventually, but I want you to leave."

"Know why I did what? What do you think I did besides try to help you?"

"Oh, that's rich! Do you think showing me the sights and giving me a few orgasms helped me? I don't need your help or my siblings' help. You can all go to hell." I jerked my arm out of his grasp. "Now, please leave."

He stared at me in complete confusion, and for just a second, I wondered if I was wrong, but I knew I wasn't. I took another step back. "I'm sorry you came all the way here, but I think it would be better if you left."

"I'll leave after you answer two questions."

I crossed my arms over my chest, clenching my jaw to avoid falling into his arms. "What?"

"Why did you leave Lake Tahoe without saying goodbye?"

"Why? You know the answer to that question!" I snapped. "You were only with me because my brothers put you up to it."

"What the hell are you talking about?" His voice grew louder with anger. "I was with you because I wanted to be with you."

"Bullshit, Landan! I heard you all talking!"

"Talking? Talking about what?"

"I already answered two questions. You need to leave now."

He stared at me, then shook his head while he looked around. "Let me help you clean this place up."

"Landan, I do not need or want your help. You have done enough."

His brows popped. "I've done enough? If you think I have done enough, then maybe you will answer one more question."

I huffed. "Fine, if I promise to answer one more question, will you leave?"

"Yes, after you answer this question, I'll go if you still want me to."

"I want you to leave, no matter the question." He stared at me for a long moment, and I forced myself to keep my eyes locked on his. "Well?"

"Coral, was any of it real?"

I jerked back slightly. "Are you talking about my time in Lake Tahoe or these bullshit charges that I have hanging over my head."

"Coral, I know those aren't real. I am talking about us. I am talking about what we had in Lake Tahoe. Was any of that real?"

I blinked a few times and wanted to tell him it was all real for me, but what would that give me besides more heartache? I slowly met his gaze again. "No."

"No?"

"That's what I said, Landan. Now, will you please leave? There is nothing here for you."

He looked like I had just kicked him in the gut, and I wondered if I was wrong about him. Maybe he had been telling me the truth about how he felt. Maybe my siblings had put him up to it, but then he realized he did like me.

He nodded slowly. "So, that's it, huh?"

"Yes," I said quickly, trying to hide the shake in my voice.

He turned and looked around again, then glanced at me. "For what it is worth, it was real to me, Coral, and I might not have anything here for me, but if you ever decide that you want to own up to the truth about your feelings, then you know where to find me."

"I am being truthful," I said, but my voice lacked the conviction I had intended to use.

He clenched his jaw and, in three steps, was in front of me. "No, you are lying." Before I could respond, Landan took hold of my face and kissed me so fiercely that I wasn't sure if he was branding or punishing me. There was no way to deny him, and I opened my mouth to participate in the kiss.

A few seconds later, Landan pulled back and tipped my face up to his, staring into my eyes. "I told you that you were lying, Coral. When you are ready to face the truth about everything, you come and find me. I'll be waiting for you because I know we are meant to be together. I'll wait for you to come home because you were meant to be there with me. I feel it in every cell of my body. I wasn't lying about anything I said to you. Come to me when you are ready."

His gaze landed on my lips again, and I thought he might kiss me, but he stepped back and dropped his hand to the side. Then he turned and walked to the door. "Don't bother keeping me up to date on your case. Thad will do that." He stepped out of view without another word, and I stared at the empty doorway.

How did he know my attorney? I thought back on our brief conversation and didn't recall saying his name. The way he had said that was like he personally knew the man.

I leaned back against the table behind me. Holy crap! Did Landan know the attorney? Was Landan paying for my lawyer?

There was no way he would have done that. I grabbed a broom and began to sweep up the mess, but in the back of my mind, I wondered. If Landan didn't care about me, would he have come here? Wouldn't he have come to my arraignment and not sent his sister if he had cared? But why had Luna been there?

Then I remembered that Landan had been heading to Canada on business. Is that why Luna came? To keep him updated? I circled back to a previous question: Did Landan know my attorney?

I shoved the broom into the corner and went to grab my jacket and purse, and then I ran out of the café, stopping only long enough to lock the front door behind me. I jumped in my car and drove straight to my brother's house. The roads were slippery and took more patience than I had, but I arrived in one piece.

Evan answered the door when I knocked—okay, more like banged on it.

"She lives," he grunted when he pulled it back and held it open.

I stepped in and turned to him. "I need to ask you a question."

"What?"

"Did you and Alaina hire my attorney?"

"Nope, we had nothing to do with it."

"Who hired my attorney, Evan?"

"I think you already know."

"I want you to say it, Evan."

"The same person who put up the million-dollar bail."

"Who, Evan?"

Alaina's voice broke the tension in the hallway. "Landan did, Coral. Before I could do anything, Landan had already jumped in and taken care of it."

Now I felt like I had been kicked in the gut. What man would do that for a woman that he didn't honestly care about? I closed my eyes and sank back to the stairs behind me, covering my face with my hands. What had I done? Oh, shit! What had I done?

CHAPTER TWENTY-SEVEN

LANDAN

I stayed in town overnight just in case Coral changed her mind. I knew she could contact Tim and get my information if she wanted to speak to me.

I lay in bed that night, tossing and turning and wondering if I had been wrong about her. Maybe I had just been a good time to her. Perhaps I made more out of our short relationship than she had. What if the words she said to me were a lie or spur-of-the-moment feel-good comments that had no meaning behind them?

I hated to think that, but the more I considered our time together, the more it seemed possible. If Coral felt the same way I had, how could she have just up and left without so much as a goodbye? There is no way that I could do something like that to someone I truly cared about.

I slept fitfully, and the next morning, I was up early and changed my flight to leave around noon. I stayed at the hotel as long as possible, then left to drive back to Harrisburg.

The entire way back, I felt like a mule had kicked me in the head. My thoughts were scattered. I tried to keep thoughts of her out of my mind, but they kept appearing out of nowhere. Every moment that we shared played repeatedly.

When I arrived home late that night, all I wanted was a drink, a shower, and to pass out in bed.

It wasn't until the next day that I let my mother know I was back in town. She asked one question. "Are you alone?"

"Yeah," was my soulful reply.

"I know you don't want to hear this, but you will get over Coral in time."

"I hope so, Mom. Because I have never felt this lost in my life. Not even after Eve."

"I'm so sorry, honey. I wish there were something I could do."

"I do, too," I told her and then changed the subject.

I threw myself into my work and bounced around the country. About a week before Christmas, Thad called, and it was the first time I heard her name mentioned to me since I had spoken to my mother when I got home from my ill-fated trip to Pennsylvania.

"I thought you might want to know; they dropped the charges on Coral."

"They did? Why?"

He laughed. "Why? Because she was innocent."

"That's not what I meant. I knew Coral was innocent. What finally persuaded them to believe it?"

"The box they recovered had physical evidence linking her assistant manager to it."

"What about the box? I don't know anything about it."

"Coral had received a box the month before that had been damaged. Not only that but it had been opened and then retaped. They tested the tape and found fingerprints and DNA under it that were Monica's."

"But what does that have to do with Coral being innocent?"

"Because Monica was having the drugs added to the shipment, and she was turning it over to her boyfriend, who is in a motorcycle gang in the area."

"Are you serious?"

"Yes, and when they found out she had been arrested, they quickly sent money to Coral's account to make it look like she was involved. She wasn't."

"I knew she wasn't."

"I did, too. There is no way a woman like that could have been involved with something like that. You have good taste. I'm surprised she didn't tell you all this."

"I haven't spoken to Coral in a while."

"You haven't? I thought you two were a couple."

"It's complicated."

"Do you want me to send her my bill?" he asked, and I laughed.

"No. You'll give the woman a heart attack. I know she could never afford your services. As far as I know, she thinks her brother and sister-in-law are footing the bill."

"I'm not so sure of that."

"Why? Did she say something to you?"

"Not about the bill, but she did tell me to give you a message, which I thought was weird at the time."

My heart began to beat harder. "What did she say?"

"She told me to thank you, and she is sorry."

"Sorry? Sorry about what?"

"I don't know. That is all Coral said."

"Okay, well, thank you for passing that on."

"Let me know the next time you are in my neck of the woods. We need to catch up, and you can explain all this to me."

"Yeah, I'll do that once I figure out how to explain it to myself." We shared another laugh and then hung up.

Coral was innocent, just like I knew she had been. That night, I searched her name again and found another article about how the charges had been dropped, and Monica was charged along with several men in a biker gang.

I thought about reaching out to her but realized that she knew where I was if she wanted to speak to me. I had left the ball in her court. She might have said she didn't care about me, but that kiss I had given her the last time I saw her told me otherwise.

A FEW WEEKS went by when I received a text message from Tim. *Just thought you should know that Coral sold her business and her house and packed everything she could into her car before she left town.*

I stared at his message, reading it several times before replying. *Where is she going?*

She said she needed to find herself and had no particular place in mind. However, a few of us think she might be heading west.

When did she leave?

New Year's Day. She said it was the perfect day for a new start.

That was ten days ago. Was Coral heading here? If she was, would she not be here by now? *I appreciate you letting me know. If you get news from her, please keep me updated.*

As of now, we know she is in Florida. She sends us postcards when she stops in new places. Right after he sent the message, a picture displayed a sandy beach with a sailboard in the sunset. I smiled.

Thanks for letting me know.

I'll keep you posted.

Tim was true to his word. Every week or so, he would send me a picture he had received in a group chat with all her siblings. It was always a new place. She spent several weeks in Florida, went to Alabama, then Louisiana, and then went north to Tennessee. After that, she showed up in Oklahoma before going to Texas.

I knew from Tim that she stayed in Texas for a while, visiting her sister, the one I had never met before she ventured into Colorado. I wondered if she would come to Lake Tahoe after she went to Colorado, but two weeks later, there was a postcard from Wyoming.

I thought of her often and knew eventually she would show up here. I didn't know if she would return to me or merely visit and then leave again.

I knew how much she loved this place and felt in the core of her soul that it was magical. I prayed that the magic would call her here and bring her to my doorstep. It was the only thing that kept me upbeat these days.

A few weeks later, she was in Washington State and then Oregon and I began to wonder if she would pass the lake by, or if perhaps she had already been here and gone again.

I never asked Tim questions. I merely thanked him for the update and asked how he and the family were doing.

On May thirty-first, I received another text message, and this one surprised me and made me sit up straight in my chair. Coral was now in Southern California. She had bypassed the lake. I sighed, feeling disappointed that she hadn't come back to me.

At the very least, I figured she would return to Lake Tahoe to see it in the beauty of summer. Disappointed and realizing that I needed to let her go, I sent Tim a text. *Man, I really appreciate you sending me the updates, but it is probably time to stop sending them. I need to move on.*

Understand completely, Tim replied, and I glanced over the postcard pictures he had sent again. I hoped she found what she was looking for and was happy. I was going to delete them, but something told me not to yet.

Instead, I shoved my phone into my shorts pocket and went out to meet my brother Lucas and his new girlfriend Piper for lunch.

I hadn't told my siblings about what Coral was doing. After the charges were dropped, I told them but nothing more was ever said about her. My mom knew I was missing her, but she didn't say anything.

The following day, I was on my dock with Piper and Lucas. Lucas was going to take her on a fishing trip, and we were trying to show her how to cast correctly. Lucas somehow got speared with a hook and went up to the house to clean it and put a bandage on it.

I tried to help Piper figure out what she was doing wrong and put my arms around her to show her the proper movements. She was giggling like a schoolgirl. Lucas was only thirty, and I believe she was three or four years younger than him, so not far from being a schoolgirl.

I heard Lucas laugh from the deck above. "Hey, watch it, man! She's going to hook you too!"

I laughed and turned to look back at him but froze when I saw someone standing on the rock steps at the edge of a tree.

I dropped my arms from Piper and spun around, wondering if I'd had one beer too many, but the image didn't go away. The two of us just stared at one another, and I wanted to call out her name, but my mouth was dry.

I had been dreaming of the day that I would see her again, and here she was. Beautiful with her hair pulled back in a pony-tail, wearing a peach tank top that enhanced the golden glow on her tanned arms. Her cutoff shorts stopped pretty short and gave me a great view of her sun-kissed legs.

Lucas must have noticed that I was staring at something because he leaned over the railing. Either he said, "Holy shit," because he saw her too, or because he almost fell from leaning so far. A moment later, he was running across the deck, his steps loud even from here as she started to turn away like she was going to run up the steps.

I took a few steps down the dock but saw Lucas cut her off,

his hands on her shoulders and his mouth moving quickly. He pointed his head toward us, and Piper spoke up, reminding me she was there and that Coral had just seen me with my arms around another woman.

"Who is that?"

"Coral," I said softly, watching Lucas take her arm and coax her down the steps toward me.

When they reached the dock, Lucas said, "Hey, Piper! I need your help in the kitchen."

Piper looked at me. "That's the Coral everyone talks about?"

I glanced at her and then did a double take. "They talk about her?"

She giggled again, nodding enthusiastically. "Yep. I'll leave you guys to catch up."

She practically skipped down the dock, and Coral watched her until she reached Lucas. Lucas quickly threw his arm around Piper and said loud enough that I could hear, "She's mine, not his. Go talk to him. Please, I beg you to talk to him."

Coral shifted toward me and took a tentative step. Should I let her come out here or meet her partway? I wasn't sure what would be better, and out of fear that she might flee, I remained where I was.

She locked her gaze on mine as she slowly came forward and stopped a few feet before me. "Hello, Landan. I hope you don't mind that I stopped by."

"What are you doing here, Coral?"

She hesitated like she was afraid to say something, and then she rolled her shoulders back and lifted her chin. "I'm coming home."

CHAPTER TWENTY-EIGHT

CORAL

The day after the charges were officially dropped, I decided it was time to leave. I needed a fresh start, and to do that, I had to leave Millerstown.

After all the presents were opened on Christmas Day, I told my family what I was doing.

"I have an announcement," I stated, feeling good about the decision that I had made. Ever since the night that I learned that Landan had paid for my legal fees and my bail, he had been heavy on my mind. Most of that was because I felt guilty about how I behaved.

I had also learned that night that my siblings had never been in cahoots with him to keep me busy and show me a good time. Had I stayed to listen to the conversation a bit longer, I would have known that. I could have saved us both a lot of heartbreak.

Would things have worked out between us? I don't know the answer to that, but I did know that I would eventually need to apologize to him. When that would happen, well, that was anyone's guess.

"You're going back to Lake Tahoe?" Carmen said excitedly.

"No, but I am going someplace."

"Where?"

"I am liquidating my business and putting my house on the market. I will travel for a while and figure out where I belong."

"You belong right here, silly," Evan said with a laugh.

I shook my head sadly. "No, not anymore. Ever since Mom died"—I glanced at Silvia—"please don't take this the wrong way. I am so happy for you and my father."

"I would never take offense when you speak of your mother," Silvia said sweetly.

"Thank you, but I just haven't felt right here since she passed. Something is missing, and I don't know what it is. When I was in Lake Tahoe, I felt closer to Mom than I have since she died, but maybe I will feel closer to her in other places, too. I want to take some time and figure things out. I need to find myself again, and I can't do that here."

None of my siblings responded. They all looked at one another and then my father. Whatever way he went, they would follow. My father cleared his throat and smiled tenderly. "I know you have been out of sorts with everything happening, and you, out of all my kids, have lived more of a nomad life than the rest. Your mother always used to say that you were meant for more than this town, or perhaps another town needed you more than this one does."

"So you're not upset?"

"You will be missed, Coral, but I am not upset."

"Where are you going to go?" Candy asked.

"I don't know. I'm just going to pack up my car and go. We'll see where I land."

"In Lake Tahoe, hopefully," Evan muttered.

"Maybe, but maybe not," I replied.

"When are you leaving?" Silvia asked.

"January first. What better way to start a new year than with a new journey."

"But that's only a week away," Carmen replied.

"I know, but nothing is keeping me here. I already spoke to Kayley about putting my house up, and I already have a buyer for most of my business stuff. The other things I can put in storage, and maybe one of you can oversee it when it sells."

"I'll take care of that for you," Ethan jumped in and then got up and hugged me tightly. "You will be missed, Coral, but I know you need this."

Everyone else jumped on the bandwagon, and there were tears and hugs all around, but in the end, I was at peace with my decision.

I climbed into my car at midnight as the new year began and put my car in drive. I glanced in my rearview mirror and said, "Your new life starts now. No looking back, Coral."

For months, I drove and stopped in different places. At first, I went south, where it was warm, and hoped that the sunny atmosphere would burn away thoughts of Landan, but it didn't. Seeing the clear water from the shores of Key West reminded me of the beauty of the lake and the serene feeling I had felt sitting beside him in the hot tub.

I did stay in touch with my siblings via a group chat, although I didn't say much. My input usually consisted of pictures of food and postcards I found along the way. Occasionally, I would mix the postcards up and send them out of order to keep them off track of where I was. Not that I expected any of them to come look for me, but I had a feeling that someone else was out there, not in our group chat, watching my travels.

I spent several weeks staying with my sister Cara in Texas and enjoying my niece and nephew. I found I loved Texas, and if I never found my new home, I decided to come back to Texas and be near Cara.

I didn't just drive as I went; I visited. I went to museums, took tours, hiked mountains, fished, sailed, and found new places to ski the following winter. I learned a lot about our country and even more about myself. I could be happy alone and do anything I wanted, and I had yet to find what that was. One day, I would know.

Five months to the day, I drove through Donner Pass, heading toward Lake Tahoe. There was a sense of urgency filling me, but at the same time, as I grew closer to the lake and got my first view of the beautiful mountains and the clear water, the urgency passed, and what filled me was peace. A peace that I had not known since I stood at the top of the Heavenly ski resort and thought of my mom.

For some reason, she was here with me, and I felt a warmness surround me as if she were hugging me tightly and welcoming me home. I put the windows down and inhaled the clean, fresh air feeling more content than I had in months. Perhaps this is where my mother knew I was meant to be.

I drove around the lake, and from time to time, I got out, marveling at the beauty before me and how incredibly different it was in the summer compared to the winter. This place felt like home, like I should be here and never leave. No matter what job I found to do, I knew right then that this was where I would make my new home.

But there was something else that I needed to do first. I had to resolve something else before I finally committed to being here. I continued on the road around the lake, looking for landmarks to remind me where I was going. It looked so much different in the summer, but then again, it looked the same.

I located the turnoff and slowed as his house came into view. His gate was open, and his Expedition was out front, but another car was there too. He had company. What if it was a woman? What if he had moved on?

If that was the case, I would thank him for what he had done for me and apologize, and then I would wish him well and leave. Not leave the area. I was staying. It might be a close-knit area, but I knew there was room for both of us. If anything, we might end up being good enough friends that we could go skiing together occasionally.

I found the courage to drive into his driveway and stopped the car. The landscaping around his property was gorgeous, and as I approached the door, I heard laughter around the back. I skimmed the house and started down a long set of stone steps. Several trees blocked my view, but eventually, I stepped around one and stopped.

There was Landan. He was out on the dock wearing shorts and a T-shirt. His hair tussled by the wind, and my heart sighed, but only for a second as I realized there was a woman with him giggling, and he wrapped his arms around her.

When I realized that, I heard Lucas talking on the deck, and I feared moving in case either of them noticed me. But Landan saw me, and he began to move forward. Fear had me spinning on the steps and heading back up. I couldn't talk to him if he was with another woman. I just couldn't.

Before I could reach the top, Lucas practically landed on me and grabbed my arms. "Where do you think you are going?"

"I can't talk to him when he is with someone else. This was a bad idea."

"Landan isn't with anyone else, Coral. Are you kidding me? He can't stop thinking about you!"

"You're wrong, Lucas. He's down there with a woman right now."

He laughed. "Coral, that's my girlfriend, Piper. He's trying to show her how to cast a line for fishing."

"Your girlfriend?"

"Yes, mine. Now, come on. I'll walk you down because you look like you are about to collapse."

"I'm fine," I stated, but he was right. My knees were shaking.

I watched Landan the entire time I came down, and it's a wonder that I didn't fall and break my neck. I think that had to do with the fact that Lucas was holding on to me so tightly.

He called for Piper and I realized as she approached that she was very young. Lucas reminded me as he walked away that Piper was his, not Landan's.

I stopped a few feet away from him. "Hello, Landan. I hope you don't mind that I stopped by."

His voice wasn't cold when he spoke, but it wasn't altogether friendly either. "What are you doing here, Coral?"

The words took a moment, but I pulled my shoulders back and faced him before I finally said, "I'm coming home."

"Coming home? I don't understand."

I wrung my hands for a moment. "I am sure that it sounds odd to you, but I have been driving around the country looking for a place that would feel like home to me. It wasn't until I returned here and saw the lake and the mountains again that I realized this is where I should be."

"How long have you been here?"

"A couple of hours. I stopped a few times to take in the view of the lake." I pulled my gaze from his and skimmed it over the water. "It is even more gorgeous in the summer."

"What brought you here, Coral? To my house?"

I shuffled forward a little. "I wanted to thank you for all you did for me. I didn't know that you had hired Thad or paid for my bail. I had no idea until the day you left the café."

"How did you figure it out?"

"Because you called him Thad. I knew I hadn't mentioned his name. I went over to Alaina's and Evan's and asked them if they had hired him, and they told me it was all you."

He shrugged. "Okay, so you thanked me. You're welcome. I'm glad that things turned out for you."

"Me, too."

We continued to stare at one another. "Is there anything else you wanted to say to me?"

I gnawed on my bottom lip, afraid to utter the words but

knowing I needed to do it. If Landan said it was too late, I would thank him again and walk away with my head held high.

"I lied to you."

"When?"

"When you came to the café. I told you that I didn't care and that I didn't have feelings for you. I did. I truly did, but the night of your party, I overheard you talking to my brothers, and it sounded like I was a joke. I thought my family had talked you into spending time with me to make me have a great vacation."

"What? They never did that."

"I know that now, but I only heard part of the conversation that night, and I was so upset that I couldn't get out of here fast enough. I thought I had made a fool of myself, and the last thing I ever expected was for you to show up in Millerstown. It threw me for a loop, and I was going through so much that I couldn't deal with it."

His brow furrowed slightly, and he glanced around.

"So that's why I told you I didn't have feelings for you."

He stepped forward. "I remember the conversation now, and perhaps if you heard only a few words, you might have concluded that they were up to something, but I don't think you heard the part about how happy you made me and how much I enjoyed spending time with you. Coral, I wasn't joking when I told you I was falling in love with you."

The air in my lungs burned as I held it for a few seconds, then it burst out with a question I had to know the answer to. "Do you still feel the same way, Landan?"

CHAPTER TWENTY-NINE

LANDAN

"Do I still feel like I am falling in love with you?" I asked her to clarify what she wanted to know. "I honestly don't know. It has been over six months since we were together, Coral. Do I still have feelings for you? Yes, I do. Are they enough for us to get over this? I'm not sure. I think that depends on you."

"On me? What do you mean?"

"Are you here to stay, or are you just visiting and planning to get back on the road?"

"I just told you that I am coming home, Landan. You told me when I was ready to come back to you, to come home. I'm here now and want us to see if we can build something. That is if you haven't already moved on."

I stepped forward slowly, studying her bright eyes and hopeful expression. "No, I haven't moved on, Coral. I wanted to, but I couldn't. Tim has been keeping me updated on where you were, and when I heard you went from Oregon to Southern California, I thought it was too late. I figured you had decided not to come back or had been here already but didn't want anyone to know that you had."

"I was in Southern California about four weeks ago. I went from there to Oregon, then Washington, stopped in Utah, and then came here. I sent the cards out of order so people would think I was avoiding this place, but this was my final destination all along. I knew that when I left Millerstown. I just needed time to myself. Time to find out who I was and figure out what I wanted out of life."

"Did you find yourself?"

She smiled, her eyes sparkling in the sunshine. "I think I did."

"And what are you planning on doing with yourself now?"

She laughed. "Well, I don't want to own a business again. That's too much stress, and I'm not sure exactly what I want to do, but I was hoping to find a job at one of the ski resorts during the winter and possibly work someplace in retail during the summer. I know it's not glamourous or anything, and you probably want someone more professional—"

I didn't let her finish the sentence because I took hold of her face and pulled her forward, plastering her body to mine and ravishing her mouth. When I finally pulled back, I ran my fingers over her sun-kissed cheeks. "I want you. I don't want anyone different than you, Coral."

"Are you sure, Landan?"

"I can't promise anything, but what I can tell you is that I want to see if this can work. That's all I have ever wanted."

"Okay, then that's what I want too."

I took her hand. "Let's have a seat. I can feel you shaking."

"Yeah, I was a little nervous when I arrived, and when I saw you with your arms around another woman, I thought my chances were zero and you had moved on."

I led her to the end of the dock, and we sat side by side. For a few moments, neither of us spoke. Her eyes shifted slowly over the lake, and I watched her inhale deeply a few times, releasing each breath slowly.

"There were times that I wanted to move on, but then Tim

would send me a new postcard picture, and I would have hope again."

"I'm sorry for how I acted and for leaving without saying goodbye or explaining. I was so overwhelmed by what I felt for you, and what I heard made me think you were only spending time with me because they asked you."

"No one ever asked me to spend time with you, Coral. I felt drawn to you when I saw you standing by the water the night you arrived."

"You saw me that night?"

I nodded. "I did. You were standing there as if you were trying to lose yourself in the scenery, and I wanted to come ask you what was wrong. Then I saw Silvia with you and wondered if you were mourning someone."

"Maybe I was mourning my life because I was concluding that it wasn't turning out as planned. I wasn't sure what I wanted or needed to do anymore. I haven't felt close to my siblings in years, and here they were, all getting married and starting families. I didn't have any prospects, and since I can't have children, I wasn't really looking because I didn't want to let anyone down."

"Coral, just because you can't have kids, that shouldn't let someone down. If they love you enough, you will be enough for them."

She asked, "Do you think I could be enough for you?"

"I do, but I hope that you would consider adopting if things work out for us."

"I would. For you, I most definitely would."

I took her hand and kissed the back. "What do you think of the lake now that you have seen it in the summer?"

"It is stunning. Utterly incredible. I could sit here all day and stare out over the calm water."

"Yeah, I have often lost track of time doing just that. Wait till you see what it looks like from the center of the lake. It is amazing how clear the water is and how far you can see down."

She turned to me. "Will you take me out on the water?"

I leaned forward and cupped her cheek. "I will take you anywhere your heart desires, Coral."

She met me in the center, and we kissed slowly and tenderly. As I pulled back, I felt all the feelings I had been trying to deny shimmer to the surface again. Coral was home, and I wouldn't let her leave again quite so easily.

CHAPTER THIRTY

CORAL

I had been in Lake Tahoe for eight weeks. I felt more alive and happier than I could ever remember feeling. For the first few days after my return, I stayed at a small hotel not far from his house, but on the fifth day, Landan showed up at my door early in the morning and told me to pack my things.

At first, I had been confused, wondering if he had changed his mind about us, but he hadn't. He told me instead that he couldn't live another day without me by his side at night. He wanted to wake up with me beside him, and fall asleep with me in his arms.

A week after I arrived, he took me up the mountain at Heavenly on the gondola, and then we hiked the rest of the way to the top. We had a picnic as we looked down from almost ten thousand feet up. It was the most incredible moment of my life, and I knew I would keep having those wonderful moments.

I could feel my mother all around me, and when Landan looked at me and said he loved me and never wanted to be without me, I felt my mother coaxing me to reciprocate the words. It wasn't hard because I knew I was in love with him.

Landan had another surprise for me that made the day even

better. After we ate, he got on one knee. "The moment I saw you skiing ahead of me, and you looked back over your shoulder and smiled, was the day that I began to fall in love with you. Only hours later, I began to see a future with you. Even though we hadn't known each other long or well, I knew we were meant to be. When you left without saying anything, I thought I had lost what I had always dreamed of having, but here you are. You're back, and things are even better than I could have ever wished them to be." He kissed the back of my hand before he continued. "I fell in love with you, and I want to spend the rest of my life beside you, showing you how much you mean to me. I want you to be my wife, Coral. Will you marry me? Will you spend your life with me here in this Heavenly place?"

"Yes!" That was all I could say before I threw my arms around him and pulled him to the blanket we were sitting on. Landan and I made love at the top of that Heavenly place, and then we lay there staring at the beautiful ring he had given me.

So here I was eight weeks later, standing in front of a mirror, awed by the beautiful white dress I wore and the flowers woven into my hair by Luna. I could hear our guests' excited and happy chatter outside near the lake edge.

My father stepped into the room, his eyes tearing up as he came to stand behind me. "You are gorgeous, Coral. I wish your mother were here to see you."

"Don't worry, Dad, she can see me. She's been with me the whole time I have been here."

He smiled, and I turned and stepped into his arms. "He makes you happier than I have ever seen you."

"He does, and I think I do the same to him."

"I'm proud of you." He stepped back and studied me. "For a while, I wasn't sure if you would ever make your way back here, but Silvia assured me that you would. She said you needed time to find yourself, and then you would find the man you should be with for the rest of your life."

"That is precisely what I did."

"I know," he replied with a tender smile. "Well, I'll let you finish getting ready, and I'll be waiting for you downstairs when it's time." He paused. "You aren't having second thoughts, are you?"

"Not even one, Daddy. Landan is the man I want to be with for the rest of my life."

"Then I pray you two will have a wonderful, long, happy life together."

He hugged me again, then kissed my cheek gently before leaving the room. As he left, all three of my sisters rushed inside. While I had chosen light blue as my wedding colors, their dresses were different. I had left it up to them to pick what they wanted to wear. Behind them was Luna, smiling widely. Her light-blue dress was the most elegant of them all. She winked at me.

My sisters were my bridesmaids, but Luna was my maid of honor. Since I arrived back in Lake Tahoe, the two of us had grown very close. So close that when she told me she was opening a unique spa and boutique here, she asked me to manage it, and I jumped at the chance, although I did tell her I would need extra time off in the winter for skiing. She told me I could only have the time off if she could join me.

Her boutique had opened two weeks ago and was a hit. Using her new skincare line, we offered all kinds of facials, nails, and skin treatments, and believe it or not, nose hair conditioning was one of the most popular with the male clientele.

I was also getting very close to Lucy and London, Landan's parents, and Lucas, who recently moved back to the lake to live in the family home year-round. I had seen the rest of the siblings, except Laney, on and off as they came to visit, but their lives kept them busy in other places.

"It's almost time," Cara said to me before she went to stand at the door overlooking the lake. "I just can't get over how incredible it is here."

I was so glad that my oldest sister and her husband were able to join us here. Since we weren't in Pennsylvania, it was safe for them to attend the wedding. "I told you that you would love it. You and Bryan must stay with us in the summer with the kids."

"What about us?" Carmen asked, bouncing her six-week-old daughter in her arms as she asked.

"You are all invited," I told her.

"Do we get to stay at the guesthouse?" Candy queried.

"You might be able to. Landan and I are talking about making that our main house, but we will keep the North Shore house for special occasions or rent it out to friends."

"That's perfect, but isn't the guesthouse a little big for you two alone?"

"We won't be alone very long," I stated, and Cara turned to look back at her sisters, then me.

"If you were anyone else, I would say that you were talking about having a baby, but we know you can't."

"You're right. I can't, but that won't stop Landan and me from having a family. We have already contacted an adoption agency and are waiting for the final word, but we think that in about a month, we might have a new addition to our family."

"Holy smokes!" Candy stated. "You're going to adopt so soon? But you guys are only now getting married. Don't you want to enjoy married life first?"

"We will get plenty of time to enjoy married life, but neither of us is that young." I pointed to her stomach, which showed signs of a baby bump. "It's not like you waited long after your wedding to get pregnant."

"Yeah, well, you're right. With everyone else having kids, I felt left out," Candy stated.

I glanced at Luna. "You know, you're next."

She laughed. "The hell I am! I have no intention of getting nailed down and impregnated by some fool."

We all cracked up, and then Luna stepped forward. "It's almost time. Are you ready for your veil?"

"Do I need to wear that thing?" I asked her. I wasn't interested in it, but she had pressured me, stating that Landan would love it.

"Yes, you need to wear it. The rest of you should go downstairs, and we will be there in a minute."

My sisters each took a moment to hug me and tell me they loved me. For the first time in a long time, I felt their love as if I belonged in that family again. I watched them head out as Luna turned me around to face the mirror.

"Landan has dated many women in his years, but I have never seen him look at a woman the way he does you."

"How does he look at me?"

"Like you are the air he breathes."

I smiled. "No, that's just the Lake Tahoe air."

She chuckled and placed the veil upon my head. "Welcome to the family, Coral. I'm so happy to have a new sister as incredible as you."

She held me tightly for a moment, then smoothed my dress and handed me my bouquet of wildflowers that grew on the mountainside nearby. She had hired someone personally to acquire them just for my wedding.

If there was one thing I had learned about this family, they stopped at no expense to have what they wanted but weren't frivolous with their money. They spent it wisely and enjoyed what they spent it on.

Luna and I walked down the stairs of her parents' house, and I could hear music being played outside by the musicians.

"Are you ready?" my father asked.

"Yes, I am ready."

Lance and Levi brushed kisses over my cheeks before they began to walk Silvia and Lucy down the aisle to their seats.

One by one, my sisters slowly emerged into view of the guests, and then it was Luna's turn. "I love you like you were my blood sister." She winked and then spun and walked toward the door to the outside.

I blinked back tears, overwhelmed by her words, but then my father took my arm. "Are you nervous?"

"Not at all, Daddy."

"Then all is right."

The music changed, and we stepped forward into the beautiful summer sun. We took our time going down the front stairs and then over the red carpet that led from the front of the house to the area beside the lake where the nuptials would take place.

Before me were a sea of guests, and at first, I couldn't see Landan. All I could see were people. Friends of his, new friends of mine, my siblings, their spouses, the Youngs were all here, and there was his huge family and more people I didn't know.

Finally, I got to the point where I could see Landan and, behind him, the view of the water and the breathtaking mountains of Lake Tahoe. As I continued to step forward, the peace I now associated with my mother washed over me, and I knew she was there with me. She was happy for me.

My father handed me off to Landan, who quickly wiped his cheek. Before the pastor, Landan and I said our vows. We swore to love each other and always be there for each other. We vowed to protect one another and continue to build a wonderful life together.

As the sun shimmered over the water, Landan slipped the ring on my finger, as I did to him, and then he gave me an intense kiss, but so tender that I felt it in my toes.

When the pastor introduced us as Mr. and Mrs. Landan Lancaster, I giggled and couldn't help but throw my arms around Landan. Instead of walking down the aisle, Landan scooped me up and carried me.

I glanced back at the water as I went and noted at least a dozen boats that had pulled close to shore to witness our wedding. "I love you, Landan Lancaster."

"And I love you, Mrs. Landan Lancaster."

Behind us, his family and mine mixed as they followed us on the path to start our life together.

The End

SNEAK PEEK: LEO, LOVING A LANCASTER, BOOK 1

Chapter One - Heather

"Welcome to Reno," the flight attendant said over the loudspeaker. Terry giggled and began playfully stomping her feet like a five-year-old.

"Oh my god! We finally made it!" She undid her seat belt, and I frowned.

"We aren't even to the gate yet, Terry. You aren't supposed to take that off until we get there and the plane stops."

"Don't be such a mother! You're on vacation!" She rolled her eyes as she spoke and then messed with her phone. After punching a few buttons, her cell phone started alerting her to notifications. "I am ready to get off this damn plane and go have fun."

I raised a brow, glancing over the seat at the rows before us. "Terry, we are in row twenty-two. Do you see all those people seated in front of us? They have to get off first."

She looked at me as if surprised. "No, we don't have to wait. I mean, we could push our way through."

She returned her attention to her phone as another notification sounded, and she huffed. "We just landed, and Todd has already sent me six texts asking me if we are there yet."

"We are not pushing our way through the crowd," I told her. "We are going to wait our turn."

"Spoilsport." She pouted and started typing on her phone as I sighed, rested my head against the seat, and looked out the window beside me.

Outside, I couldn't see much, but I saw enough to know I wasn't in Ohio anymore. There were no mountains in central Ohio, but I could see some off in the distance here, and I looked forward to seeing them up close for the next week.

Terry's phone alerted again, and I figured I should probably let my mom and the kids know I had at least landed. I retrieved my phone from my purse and turned off the airplane mode. Unlike Terry, I didn't have a ton of messages from my husband or friends. I didn't even have one message, but that was alright. I had gotten used to that.

I opened up the group message I had started with my mother, Tim, and Charlotte—or Charlie, as she preferred—and typed, *Landed in Reno.*

I skimmed over my email while I waited for us to taxi to the gate and saw a few emails that might need my attention later, but nothing dire.

I'm glad you arrived. Have fun. Love you, my mother responded as I closed my email, followed by a thumbs-up from Charlie. Tim didn't reply, but I didn't expect him to. Getting a sixteen-year-old boy to respond to a text was like pulling teeth on a ghost. Charlie wasn't much better, at least with me. With her fourteen-year-old friends, she would text a thousand words a minute.

I slipped my phone back into my purse and glanced at Terry, who was rolling her eyes again as she dropped her phone into her lap.

"What?" I asked.

"Nothing. Todd is such a pain. He wants me to tell him everything about my flight—like there is anything to tell. We sat down, the plane took off, I went to the bathroom, I sat back down, had a soda, and then we landed." She flopped her hand back and forth with each comment.

"Hey, be glad he is asking. He misses you."

Her brown eyes grew large. "I have been gone a whole ten hours. It's not like I have been gone for ten days."

"Be thankful someone misses you," I reiterated, shifting my head back toward the window with a weary sigh. What I wouldn't give for a few dozen texts from the man I loved.

"I am thankful," Terry continued. "Of course, I'm thankful, but man, I needed to get away. Between him and the kids, it's like I'm being smothered. I needed this vacation so badly."

Smothered was not what I would call her relationship with her family. She had three kids who adored her and a husband who worshipped the ground she walked on.

A sadness drifted over me as I remembered a time I'd had the same thing. I pushed the thoughts away and unbuckled my seat belt as the plane stopped at the gate. People started moving about, but I stayed seated, staring at the back of the seat in front of me as I recalled Paul and myself on our last vacation. We went to Aruba. Paul loved to scuba dive, and we had spent a week doing as much as we could. We came home tan and happy, and a week later, my life became unhinged.

I closed my eyes and inhaled deeply as I let the memory dissolve. Terry kept texting on her phone, standing up and then sitting down repeatedly.

"Jesus, girl, will you just relax? We will get off. Wait your turn. You are worse than a toddler with ADHD."

She snorted and eventually remained standing, impatiently tapping her elegant nails on the seat's headrest in front of her. Finally, it was our turn, and she snagged her roller bag from the overhead compartment and began to make her way down the aisle. The older man on the other side of the aisle smiled at me, and I returned it before collecting my bag and then glancing at his.

"Do you need help with that?" I asked him.

"No, but thank you so much. That is very kind of you."

I nodded and followed after Terry, who was already a good twenty feet away. She would plow through the dozen people before her if she didn't slow down.

Once in the terminal, Terry stopped outside the door, and I almost knocked her over. "What are you doing? You're in the way."

She grinned as I passed by her to make way for the people behind us. "Just taking it all in. No kids, husbands, dogs, or jobs. Just vacation with my besties."

"Speaking of besties, did you hear from the others?"

"Yeah, I had a text. They just got to the house." She lifted her phone and pulled her roller bag to catch up to me. "Look at this place!" She held the phone out to me, and I glanced at the picture of a large house.

"Can't wait to see it in person," I replied.

We navigated through the crowds and found the baggage claim quickly, but not before Terry had to throw twenty dollars in a slot machine. Of course she didn't win anything, but it made her happy to play for a couple of minutes. After we collected our bags, we walked outside, and the hot summer air slammed into me. I closed my eyes, putting my face up to the sun for a moment. A memory of Paul and me standing on a beach doing the same thing crashed over me, and I sighed.

"Why are you sighing?" Terry asked.

I forced myself to smile. "No reason. Just enjoying the sun for a moment." Even though Terry was a close friend, I didn't talk to her much about Paul. She had told me often that it was time to move on with my life.

"Well, come on, we will get a lot of time to enjoy the sun once we get to the lake."

We walked across the street to the rental car pickup location and collected our car. Terry was behind the wheel a few minutes later, and we were on the road.

For the first time since I had left, I felt excited. It wasn't that I didn't want to go on vacation. I needed one. I hadn't been away from home in three years. Without Paul, I couldn't imagine enjoying a getaway, and I wouldn't be on this trip if Terry hadn't begged me to go.

I enjoyed the sights as we drove out of Reno and toward the mountains. Terry had the music cranked up loud and sang every lyric in an off-key voice, so I didn't need to worry about talking.

As we drove around a bend, I got my first view of Lake Tahoe and smiled at the beautiful landscape. Paul would have loved to see this. Although Paul preferred to vacation on islands so he could scuba dive, he would have appreciated the view.

"There is a pull-off." I pointed, and Terry shook her head.

"You can see the lake from here. Trust me, you will get enough views once we get to the house."

I frowned but didn't say anything else. If I had been driving, I would have stopped. However, she was behind the wheel, so I was stuck doing what she wanted.

I kept my eyes focused out the window as she weaved around traffic. I saw the water glistening in the sunlight between the trees, and I put the window down. The warm summer air blew my long blond hair off my shoulders, and I smiled and closed my eyes. The window started to go back up. "What are you doing?"

"It's hot outside," Terry complained.

"It's not hot. It's perfect," I retorted and put the window back down.

"Fine," she whined, and I put my hand out the window to feel the air push against my palm as she continued driving.

A few minutes later, traffic increased significantly as we drove toward large commercial buildings. "I didn't think they had big hotels here," I said.

"Yeah, the Nevada side does because of the casinos." It didn't take long to pass those buildings, and then Terry said, "Welcome to California!"

I glanced around. "When did we cross into California?"

She thumbed over her shoulder. "At that last light. You know you're in Cali because the buildings are smaller." Unlike me, Terry had been to Lake Tahoe. She told me that they came here often on breaks when she was in college.

There were shops, restaurants, and resorts along the road, and I studied a ski lift off to the side that went way up the mountain. "There is still snow up there."

"Yeah, I think there is snow on some of them all year."

It seemed weird to have this warm air swirling around me when I could still see snow. It took a while to get through the area due to all the people, crosswalks, traffic lights, and traffic in general, but eventually, we were next to the lake again, and I enjoyed what I could see.

I had seen at least a dozen turnoffs that I would have stopped at, but Terry passed by every single one. Perhaps I could take the car out later and stop at a few by myself.

It was another twenty minutes before the GPS told her to turn off the main road, and we ended up on a narrow path toward the lake. My excitement continued to grow the closer we got to it.

As we rounded a curve, I saw an enormous house off to the right. It looked like a four-story log cabin or a small resort nestled in the woods. Out front, a few people were milling around near the garage, but I didn't pay them much attention as Terry turned to the left and another house came into view.

"Holy crap! That place is huge!" I said as I eyed the three-story house we stopped in front of. There was a long porch around the front of it and many windows. When the car stopped, I climbed out and turned to face the lake. Yes, the house was impressive, but the water view was breathtaking.

I heard a squeal behind me and several excited voices as some people came out to greet Terry, but I couldn't tear my eyes from the view. It was glorious, and the water was almost as flat as glass, which seemed surreal since I was used to the ocean, where waves were constantly rolling.

"Heather," Terry called, and I forced myself to turn away from the lake. I met her in front of the car where four women stood, eyeing me carefully. I hadn't met most of them before, as they were Terry's friends. "This is Annabell, Betsy, Corrine, and you remember Justine."

I smiled and nodded at each woman before commenting to Justine, "Of course I remember her." Justine had been one of Terry's college roommates and had remained in California after school to work in Hollywood. She was also the one who was paying for the majority of this rental because as I stood there and looked at the house behind her, I knew without a doubt that this house had to cost more than the three thousand a week that I had been told.

"Great to see you again, Heather," Justine replied, then immediately dismissed me to grab Terry's arm and pull her toward the house. "Wait till you see the inside of this place."

I followed behind the group, and my mouth dropped as I stepped through the front door and stared at the two balconies above me for the second and third floors. Yep, this place cost a lot more than Terry said.

Want to keep reading? Click here: Leo, Loving a Lancaster, Book 1

LOVING A YOUNG SERIES

The Loving a Young Series consists of six books involving the Young Siblings: Wesley, Henley, Huntley, Bradley, Riley and Kayley.

Wesley, Book 1

Traumatized by events of her past, Charlotte Bennett is not a fan of strangers. When she sees a man touching her daughter at the park, she reacts without listening. It's only later when her daughter is rushed to the hospital that she realizes how wrong she had been.

Doctor Wesley Young only wanted to help the tender-aged girl he witnessed fall, but when her mother attacks him at the park, he's left stunned. When the little girl arrives later in the emergency department, he comes face to face with the mother who makes more of an impression on him than the cut she left on his face.

Things heat up quick when Marisol is no longer his patient, but when things from the past are revealed, Wes isn't sure that Charlotte is the woman for him. Can Charlotte find a way to explain it all so that Wes will accept both her and her daughter before it's too late?

Henley, Book 2

Being a wedding planner is hard, especially when someone is always trying to steal your business, and your family doesn't support you. However, Roxanne Novak is determined to keep her business afloat.

When Roxy's in a car accident hurrying to meet a potential bride, she's injured and scared, but paramedic Henley Young takes good care of her.

Henley loves his job and thrives on the adrenaline of helping people in need. Maybe that's why when he meets Roxy, he's inclined to help her with more than just medical care. Hooking her up with his older brother Wesley and his bride-to-be could be just what she needs. It might also be the start of something between Lee and the spunky little wedding planner.

When a position at a country club is offered to Roxy, she finds herself rethinking her entire business plan. Excited to start someplace new, Roxy and Henley begin making plans for the future. Just after she starts her new job, Roxy learns of Lee's past relationship, and everything she knew about him is questioned.

Can Roxy and Henley put the past to bed and move forward to something that might be more than what both of them had ever hoped for?

Huntley, Book 3

Daniella Knight works hard to create suspenseful and romantic tales, but after a violent interaction with a fan, she wants to hide from the world. When her house catches on fire, her and her protection dog, Tigger, are forced to rely on the help of strangers.

Huntley Young loves being in the thick of the action. Well, as long as that action has something to do with his job as a firefighter. When Huntley stops the homeowner from going back into the house, he has no clue, that he just placed himself firmly in the hero department.

As they get to know each other, Daniella's creative mind is always building on what is around her, and before she knows it, reality and fiction are hard to tell apart.

When danger strikes again, will Daniella be able to see what is right in front of her, or will her past trauma keep her safely inside her romantic fictional world?

Riley, Book 4

Riley is always the life of the party, and it's Ethan that is there to pick her up and keep her together. He knows her almost as well as she knows herself, and he knows she will never love him as he does her.

Now Ethan wants more out of life and love, but Riley denies her feelings and insists they are just friends with benefits. When a training opportunity comes up that will get Ethan out of town for months, he jumps on it. It's the only way to get over Riley and move on.

With Ethan gone and a new guy in her life, Riley finds herself dealing with several emotional issues without the help of her best friend. A family emergency has Ethan feeling lost without Riley there to lean on, but he refuses to go to her and seeks solace with another.

Will Riley make the right choices, and finally, admit how she feels, or will she find herself alone and falling further down the rabbit hole.

Kayley, Book 5

Independent Kayley Young is a real estate agent in New York and loves her life as a single woman. She's not one to get tied down, and she has no desire to have children.

Officer Cameron Sexton is new on the job, a veteran of the military, and proud of his dedication to the job. Unfortunately, he finds himself annoyed at his lackadaisical sergeant who should hang up his gun belt before getting someone hurt. When Cameron is dispatched to a burglary, he meets Kayley Young and is instantly attracted to her. Cameron has a feeling she reciprocates those feelings, except she's a little leery of the fact that he is ten years younger than her.

When Kayley's life starts taking a turn for the worse, she finds herself depending more on the attractive young man she has let into her bed for fun than she intended. Her original thought of enjoying the moment starts to last longer, but Kayley's not sure that dating a man ten years her junior is smart for the long haul. Especially with the rest of the changes that have happened in her life.

Can Kayley come to terms with the age difference, or will her family sway her away from the younger man?

Bradley, Book 6

Bradley Young is the eldest sibling of the Young family, and the only one who had previously been married. After losing his wife to cancer several years ago, he's used to caring for his two kids alone. The thought of dating is not something he's interested in, now with a busy construction business, and a family that always needs help.

Nolan Nickels needed a change, and with the help of her good friend, Kayley, she left New York and came to Millerstown to take a teaching position at the middle school. She has always been a huge tom boy and loves to fix things with her hands and play sports.

With a new house in her name, Nolan seeks out the perfect plan to get the house ready so she can bring her two daughters' home, but is her fixer-upper more than she bargained for? When Kayley finally gets Brad to stop by the house to check something, Brad finds himself more than intrigued with the spitfire, Nolan. Will he finally find the woman to spend his life with, or will she be put a halt on any type of future?

The *Loving a Winston Series* is a five-book steamy romance series that spins off of the *Loving a Young Series*. Characters from both series will appear from book to book. Each book is a standalone romance with suspense and spicy romance scenes.

LOVING A WINSTON SERIES

T he *Loving a Winston Series* is a five-book steamy romance series that spins off of the *Loving a Young Series*. Characters from both series will appear from book to book. Each book is a standalone romance with suspense and spicy romance scenes.

Cara, Book 1

What happens when the man you fall for is all wrong for you?

Cara Winston has always been a bit of a rebel and an adrenaline junkie. As a helicopter pilot and paramedic, she relies on that to do her job.

When Cara and her team respond to a multi-vehicle accident involving motorcycles, she's expecting the worst. What she's not expecting is to find herself intrigued by the blue eyes of a man wearing motorcycle gang colors.

Ryan Vigilante rides the road, mostly on two wheels, not four. When several of his club end up in an accident on the highway, Ryan never expects to see a future in the eyes of the intense female paramedic. The only problem is, she's way out of his league, and he knows that getting involved with her could only put her in jeopardy.

With Cara's family trying to keep them apart and Ryan's club breaking the law, Cara finds herself more of a rebel than usual. Will things work out for Cara and Ryan, or will Cara's law enforcement brother, Ethan, find a way to put a stop to it for good?

Evan, Book 2

What happens when she's not really who you think she is?

EVAN WINSTON IS DEDICATED to his job as a registered nurse in the ICU department of the local hospital. He's one hundred percent focused on the needs of his patients and his family, or at least he usually is. That all changes the day a woman visits one of his patients and turns his world upside down.

Laney Marshall wants nothing more than to help people who struggle. Especially those women and children who are fighting to survive domestic violence situations. After losing someone close to her to an abusive man, she is determined to do everything in her power to help.

Unfortunately, Laney has people that don't want her to do that. In fact, they don't even want her in this town or even the state of Pennsylvania. They prefer her on the other side of the country, where they think she belongs, living the life planned for her.

Can Laney and Evan find a way to build a relationship while keeping others from getting involved, or will the revealed secrets be enough to end any chance of a future before it begins?

. . .

Candy, Book 3

What happens when your lustful heart wins over your intellectual mind?

WHEN CANDY'S SISTER, Cara, was dating outlaw biker member Ryan Vigilante, Candy paid little attention to Ryan's club buddy, Bollard. Sure, Bollard, who works behind the bar at the local tavern, was pleasing on the eyes and made a mean chocolate martini, but he was an outlaw, and that's not the kind of person Candy associates with.

Michael Bollard is out of the club now, and he hopes to purchase the tavern. He had never wanted anything more than his bikes and the club, but now, Mike has hopes of building a future, a future that is colliding with sexy and intelligent Candy Winston in ways he could have never imagined.

Just when he thinks he might have his future figured out, a stranger enters the bar with a surprise he never saw coming. Will that surprise send Candy running for higher ground, or will it cement her future in the tavern with Mike?

Carmen, Book 4

What happens when your first love returns to town—twenty years later?

CHILD PSYCHOLOGIST, Carmen Winston, spends a lot of time at the schools, and when she come across a man and the name of a new student, she is thrown back to a time of young love and dreamy hopes of the perfect future.

Tim Kohl lived in Millerstown for six years before his

parents moved him across the country. He never expected to return, and when he does, it's with three kids in tow. The last thing he expects to find in town is his high school sweetheart still beautiful as ever and single.

When sparks fly, can these two put the past behind them and plan a future, or will the years apart separate them before they can figure it out.

Coral, Book 5

What happens you overhear your family talking to the man you've fallen for?

CORAL WINSTON HAS FELT out of touch with her family since her mother passed away and throws everything she has into her coffee café. When her family forces her to take a vacation, they all decide to come along for the fun.

Landan Lancaster is the oldest of the eight Lancaster children, and he's still trying to deal with walking away from his cheating bride the night before their wedding many months prior. When a large family comes to stay in the Lancaster guest house on the lake, he finds himself intrigued by the woman standing at the water's edge.

On the slopes, Landan realizes he has met his match in more ways than one, and Coral begins to feel as if she has finally found where she belongs. When a conversation is overheard, Coral gets the wrong idea and flees, only to find a mountain of trouble waiting for her back home.

Can Coral overcome the issues facing her and find her way back to the beautiful mountains and water of Lake Tahoe, or will Landan lose her before he can ever call her his own?

LOVING A LANCASTER SERIES

The Loving a Lancaster Series spins off of the Loving a Winston Series. In Coral's book, you are introduced to the Lancaster family while she is on vacation in Lake Tahoe. This series will consist of seven books, and stared with Leo.

Leo - Book 1

Leo Lancaster is coming home to Lake Tahoe. As a successful stockbroker and business owner, Leo has decided to open another office in Truckee and work out of that one instead of his Vegas office. Now, he must locate a house and get himself settled, and the last thing he expects to find on his return is love.

Heather McClain is a devoted mother of two teens, and a widow from Ohio. When her best friend encourages her to go on a girls trip to Lake Tahoe, she decides to take a break from the chaos at home and try to have fun. Only their antics are more than Heather bargained for.

Lucky for her, Leo is around to rescue her and the two of them quickly grow close, but is Heather ready to let go of her husband's memory and move forward into a relationship, or more importantly, are her children prepared to accept a new man into their mother's life when she surprises them with a trip to the lake?

Luna - Book 2

WHILE LUNA LANCASTER loves Lake Tahoe, she thrives in the outdoors near her home in Sedona, Arizona. When Luna's good friend, Sadie, plans a visit and decides to bring a guest, Luna is excited to show them the sights of the beautiful Red Rocks around her home.

Unfortunately, Luna's friend can't make it at the last minute, and Luna finds herself entertaining Trace Hampton alone. The chemistry between them sparks the moment they meet. The problem is that Luna thinks Trace and Sadie are a couple, and she does everything possible to hide her feelings and not act on them.

When Trace reveals that he is not involved with Sadie, Luna jumps at the chance to see what they could have, but when Sadie finds out, she's heartbroken that Luna stole the man she likes out from under her.

Will Luna save the friendship and lose the chance at a happily ever after with Trace?

Levi, Book 3

LEVI LANCASTER IS the youngest of the family, and while not as classy and outgoing as his older siblings, he works hard for his own HVAC company.

When a major snowstorm hits Lake Tahoe, Levi is enlisted to do a favor and finds himself quite taken with Diane Hampton. He's heard of her through his sister, Luna, and Luna's boyfriend, Trace, but he has never had the chance to meet them.

Diane loves her new life in Lake Tahoe, but she is not a fan of driving in the snow. When Levi comes to help her out, Diane may find herself finally ready to move on after the loss of her fiancée five years ago.

When a stranger arrives at the lake and tries to insert herself into Levi's life, Diane tries to figure out if the woman is after something, or just trying to find pieces of her past. Can Diane protect Levi or will he push her away when she is only trying to help?

Life is about to change for these two, but will it be for the better?

Still to come: Lance, Lily, Laney, and Lucas.

LOOKING FOR ANOTHER STEAMY SERIES?

I f you are looking for another steamy series, make sure to check out the Pleasure Your Fantasies Series! This series consists of the following books: Mistletoe Fantasies, Book 1 - Whispered Fantasies, Book 2 - Secret Fantasies, Book 3, Conflicted Fantasies, Book 4, Returning Fantasies Book 5, Discovered Fantasies, Book 6, Arrested Fantasies, Book 7 (releasing in 2025) - Plus Two more that haven't been written yet!

Mistletoe Fantasies, Book 1, Pleasure Your Fantasies Series
Reba

I RELEASED a hefty sigh as I dropped my stage persona and passed through the garnet velvet curtain for the final time that night. I was always thankful when my dancing shift ended. It wasn't that I hated to dance; I did enjoy it—kinda—okay, sometimes. The money was good—like, seriously damned good. That was what had enticed me to do it in the first place. I sure as hell wasn't a fan of strutting my stuff on the runway for the exclusive clientele. Of course, if there was any place where I *had* to be a dancer, I was glad that it was at Pleasure Your Fantasies and that Quinn Monroe was my boss.

I leaned against the wall with one shoulder and unhooked my five-inch platform heels as I pondered my sexy-as-sin elusive boss. Mr. Quinton Monroe ran a tight ship. He demanded respect not only from his employees and clients, but he expected his clients to have the utmost respect for his employees, especially his dancers.

Mr. Monroe also required his employees to be professional and care for themselves mentally and physically. He didn't allow employees with emotional issues or bad habits to remain unless they received help or kicked the habits. Mr. Monroe would give them a chance because he was a fair man, but if they couldn't deal with therapy or the process of getting clean or—god forbid —remaining that way, then he kicked their asses to the curb. He had more important things to do, and I didn't blame him.

All the employees knew the score when hired: They signed contracts that gave explicit instructions on what would happen should they be found to have emotional or substance abuse issues. They not only signed one when hired, but then they signed it again once it was learned that they had a problem. In my opinion, Mr. Monroe was being extremely generous.

In June, Ivy had fallen off the wagon. If it hadn't been for Sophia Thayer, an ICU nurse from Celebration Township who moonlighted as a dancer, Ivy would have died from a heroin overdose. Sophia had saved her life, and while Mr. Monroe had wanted to fire Ivy that night, he hadn't. He had not only taken care of her hospital bills but paid for her rehab, too. Two weeks after she returned from rehab, he did a random drug test on her, and she failed. Ivy was escorted off the property and banned from ever returning. No one had heard from or seen her since, at least that I was aware of.

A few other dancers had come and gone, and so had other

employees from other aspects of the business. One of the bouncers, Al, was let go last month, two kitchen staff before that, and one of the trainers was fired when Mr. Monroe found he was not only using drugs but dealing them to the clients—no second chance was given to that guy.

I yawned as I made my way to the dressing room. Mr. Monroe had a very comprehensive staff that, at my last count, included over fifty people; it might have grown, though I wasn't sure. He kept his business affairs below a whisper. As far as I knew, only Ty had the boss's ear and knew the ins and outs of the business. The two of them were thick as thieves, and Ty acted as Mr. Monroe's bodyguard when needed—not that Mr. Monroe needed a bodyguard. I'd witnessed him take an unruly client down when he'd gotten out of control, and no one else was around. Mr. Monroe hadn't hesitated to put the guy against the wall, and when others had arrived, he'd straightened his coat, adjusted his tie and his cuffs, and then smiled, winked, and walked away as if nothing had happened.

I had a feeling that Mr. Monroe had several other business dealings that would explain why he was so well known in this area. When he opened this club four years ago, many people didn't think he could make it work, not when the membership was six grand a year, but Mr. Monroe ensured that his club had more than just dancers to entertain members at night. His building housed meeting rooms, places to hold conferences, a gym, a barber, saunas, a pool, hot tubs, massage services, a game room with pool and poker tables, and a smoking room. Plus, he was renovating a large section of the basement to install a wine cellar for special events.

Mr. Monroe had built a booming business, and I'd heard he was working on a similar club for women. I wondered how many men who frequented this club would allow their wives or girlfriends to join the sister club.

I gave Ty a sleepy wave as I passed him in the hall outside

the dressing room. His husky laughter followed me into the room.

"You look awfully tired for just having gotten off the stage. Normally, you look jazzed." I wanted to curl up and fall asleep at the sound of his deep, mellow voice.

"I'm beat. My neighbors were fighting all day, and I didn't get any sleep." I plopped into a chair before the mirror and grabbed the makeup remover wipes.

"That sucks. You want me to come over and have a little chat with them?" He came to stand behind me, his broad shoulders filling the mirror, his smile a bit cocky but caring at the same time. His blue eyes sparkled with mischief.

"Thank you, but no thank you. The last time you chatted with them, they put dog shit in my mailbox."

His brows slammed down, and he snarled, "You didn't tell me that."

I laughed. "Yeah, well, I forgot to mention it. It's not a big deal."

"Yes, it is. We need to find you a better place to live," Ty said as he frowned.

Ty was a sweet guy. He could be forbiddingly menacing when he wanted to be, but he was usually quiet and reserved and spent more time watching than speaking. When he felt comfortable, he'd open up and talk about anything. I'd grown to look to Ty as a big brother. That's how he made me feel sometimes, as if he would protect me from any outside threat but tease or tickle me to death if he had the opportunity.

"I will find another place once I can afford it. You know the deal." He was the only one around here that I'd confided in.

"Why don't you do a few more dancing shifts? You get great tips when you dance, much better than waitressing."

I scrunched my face. "I prefer to serve the drinks, you know that, Ty."

He laughed, picked up the light blue sweatshirt on the back

of my chair, and laid it over my shoulders. "Yeah, I know, but you could get out of that place twice as fast if you just did a few more dance shifts a month. Quinn would give them to you if you wanted them. Just say the word, and I'll make it happen." He snapped his fingers as he flashed a grin at me.

I sighed, "I'll think about it. Thanks, Ty."

He was about to say something else when Britt strutted into the room, followed by Wallie. Britt was her usual bubbly self and bounced into her seat, talking about how glad she was that the night was over.

Wallie, who never spoke—well, not around me anyway— glanced around the room as if looking for threats. After he didn't find any, he locked eyes with me in the mirror. His electric blue eyes sucked the air out of my lungs, and I couldn't move. Every time our eyes met, that occurred, and I wasn't sure what to do about it. Finally, Wallie jerked his gaze away from me and turned to Britt.

"You need anything else, Britt?" His voice was even deeper than usual, and I fought not to shiver as it slithered along my spine. He wasn't even talking to me, and I reacted that way to him. I seriously needed a night out on the town to let loose.

"Nope, I'm good, Wall. Thanks for another great night."

He nodded to her and, ever so briefly, hesitated as if he were going to say something else. He glanced my way again, spun military-style, and marched out of the room.

The moment he was gone, I could finally breathe normally again. Why was it that as soon as I saw that man, my brain began to misfire, and my lungs stopped working? Anxiety filled every cell of my body because he seemed not to like me. He joked and flirted with every other woman who stepped through the doors of this establishment. Since the day I had started over a year ago, he'd probably grunted a hundred mono-syllabic words to me, the proverbial Neanderthal.

I didn't understand it, but I supposed that in the long run, it didn't matter. I had a major crush on the guy. Even though his comments were tasteless and rude and could sometimes be construed as vulgar, something about him called to me. Deep inside, I knew that if we ever had the chance to connect, we would be perfect together, but that would never happen. Mr. Monroe didn't allow dancers to date any of the employees. He didn't care if anyone else dated. In fact, one of the waitresses was married to one of the kitchen staff, and a trainer was engaged to a masseuse. It was only taboo to date one of the dancers—yet another reason I didn't want to be a dancer, even a part-time one.

I was tired of being single. I was twenty-nine years old and wanted to find a man with whom I could fall in love and settle down. I wanted children before I was too old to have them. I didn't care that women were having kids into their forties now. I didn't want to wait that long. My heart ached every time I heard a baby cry. When I'd gone to see Pepper's baby last month, I'd cried as I held the sweet little boy in my arms. My biological clock had been ticking for the last few years, and as I approached thirty, it beat more loudly by the day.

I pulled the sweatshirt over my head and undid the bikini top that I'd worn on the stage under my sweatshirt and pulled it out my left sleeve. I tossed it into my bag to wash at home before pulling up a pair of leggings and shoving my feet into my off-brand fur-lined boots.

"Hey, you're off tomorrow, right?" Britt asked as I grabbed my down jacket and began to walk out of the dressing room.

"Yeah," I replied, praying she didn't ask me to take a shift for her.

"I'm decorating my tree and baking cookies tomorrow. Do you want to come by?"

I blinked in astonishment and wondered if I had heard her correctly. "You bake cookies?"

Britt laughed. "Yes, I bake cookies. Don't you?"

"Um, no, not normally."

Britt jumped out of her seat, and her enormous bust bounced. "Then you need to come over. I'll text you with the time when I wake up."

"Okay," I replied. I was too shocked that Britt baked to even think of saying no. Somehow, I never pictured her doing anything other than dancing. Funny, I know—because she was only at the club for eight or nine hours a night, four times a week. It was strange how little I knew about my colleagues, even stranger that the only person that I wanted to get to know was leaning against the wall in the hallway wearing a suit and wouldn't give me the time of day.

During work hours, the guards were required to wear suits, although they did not have to wear ties. Sometimes, they did, but most times they did not. Whenever I saw Wallie in a suit, it took my breath away. Okay, so fine, that happened almost every time I looked at him, but when he was in a suit, I felt the attraction even more viscerally.

As I left the dressing room, we locked eyes again. I forced myself not to look away even though I was tempted to let my eyes wander over all six-feet-one inches of him. My fingers itched to run over the top of his buzzed hair. I wanted so badly to know if his dirty blonde hair was soft or coarse on my palms so I could fantasize how it would feel between my legs. An involuntary shiver raced down my spine as I approached him.

Along with guarding Britt, Wallie was assigned to door duty, which meant he would escort me to my car. As I stopped before him, his nose flared as he inhaled sharply and stood straight, putting space between us so quickly that I leaned my nose toward my shoulder and sniffed my armpit to see if I had somehow offended him.

Without a word or another look, Wallie pushed open the door and glanced around outside. When it was clear, he held the door open. He would have taken my arm or put his hand on my lower back if I had been anyone else. I'd seen him take Britt's, Pepper's, and even Destiny's and Jewels's arms as they stepped out, but not mine. He never touched me.

I wasn't sure why, but for the first time, it really bothered me —like, seriously pissed me off—so much so that halfway through the lot, I stopped and glared at his back as he kept moving.

Wallie turned and then scanned the parking lot, looking for a threat. "Why did you stop?"

"Why don't you take my arm?"

He gave me an odd look like he thought I'd lost my mind. "What are you talking about?"

"When you escort the other girls out of the door, you take them by the arm, but you never take mine." I stalked toward him, determined to find out what his problem was. "You also don't ever talk to me, and you barely ever look at me. Why is that?"

His mouth dropped open for a second and then clamped closed. A muscle ticked in his jaw before he reached over and, none too gently took my arm. "You want me to escort you, Ms. Reba," he began to pull me toward my vehicle, stopping as he reached the side and immediately letting go of me, "then you have officially been escorted." He balled his hands into tight fists at his sides.

I wanted to scream. Had touching me been so damned horrible?

"Jesus, you're an ass, Wallie."

His blue eyes flared. "Yeah, I'm an ass. That's the safest way to think of me, Ms. Reba. Enjoy your night off."

He stalked away as a variety of feelings twisted through my gut. Why did he say that was the safest way to think of him? Why didn't he ever want to touch me? Or look at me? Or talk to me?

My mouth dropped open as I realized he knew I was off

work the next night. Either he'd been listening to my conversation with Britt or looked at my schedule. Either way, he had just shown me he was more interested than he was letting on. Now, if only there were something I could do about it. Damn—if only I could quit dancing now.

Mistletoe Fantasies, Book 1

ABOUT THE AUTHOR

Stacy Eaton began her writing career in October of 2010 and, as each year goes by, she releases more and more novels. Stacy recently took an early retirement from law enforcement after over fifteen years of service, with her last three in investigations and crime scene investigation.

Stacy resides in southeastern Pennsylvania with her husband, who works in law enforcement, and her two dogs. She has a daughter in college and a son who is currently serving in the United States Navy.

Be sure to visit www.stacyeaton.com for updates and more information on her books.

Sign up for all the latest information on Stacy's Newsletter!

Join my Newsletter and get TWO Short Stories for FREE!

STACY'S OTHER BOOKS

Rise Again Warrior Series

The *Rise Again Warrior Series* is an intense and emotional journey through the lives of many service members, their families, and their friends. Focusing on the trials that they face after wartime is over, and they have returned home to a nation that sometimes seems to have forgotten what they were fighting for, and what all of these people sacrificed in the name of Honor & Duty. Books Include: Mission: Believe, Mission:Accept, Mission: Repair, and Mission: Courage

Loving a Young Series

The *Loving a Young Series* is a steamy romance series that consists of six books. While these books are all standalone romances, the characters will be seen across the series since this is a small-town romance series about siblings finding forever loves.

Books include: Wesley, Henley, Huntley, Riley, Kayley & Bradley

The Loving a Winston Series

The *Loving a Winston Series* is a five-book steamy romance series that spins off of the *Loving a Young Series*. Characters from both series will appear from book to book. Each book is a standalone romance with suspense, adult language and spicy romance scenes.

Books Include: Cara, Evan, Candy, Coral and Carmen.

The Loving a Lancaster Series

The *Loving a Lancaster Series* spins off of the *Loving a Winston Series* when Coral Winston meets Landon Lancaster in Lake Tahoe. Characters from previously series maybe show up in these books. Each book is a standalone romance, adult language and may contain spicy romances scenes.

Books includes: Leo, Luna, Levi, Lance, Laney, Lucas, and Lilly.

The Unexpected Series

The *Unexpected Series* is a steamy romance series where anything can happen and probably will. Each book in the series is a stand-alone happily ever after, or happy for now book. While they are stand-alone, the books are all centered around Safety Zone Security and the employees there. Characters from one book will continue throughout the rest of the series. Books Include: Unexpected Packages, Unexpected Arrivals, Unexpected Trouble, Unexpected Storms, Unexpected Desires, Unexpected Ties.

Paranormal Romance:

My Blood Runs Blue Series

My Blood Runs Blue Series is an adult Paranormal Action/Romance Series with vampires and is intended for mature audiences.

Books Include: My Blood Runs Blue, The Pulse of Blue Blood, Blue Blood for Life, Mixing the Blue Blood, Blue Bloods Final Destiny,

The Return of Blue Blood Series:

This series is 40 years in the future after My Blood Runs Blue. It is a very steamy series intended for mature audiences.

Books Included: Kristin: Blue Blood Returns, Hugh: Blue Blood Compelled, Zander: Blue Blood Reborn, Lena: Blue Blood Desired, Reckoning, Blue Blood Finale

Single Titles

Whether I'll Live or Die

You're Not Alone

Garda ~ Welcome to the Realm

Liveon ~ No Evil

Second Shield

Distorted Loyalty

Six Days of Memories

Second Shield II: The Return

Tempt Me Too

Finding the Strength

Finding Love in Special Places:

Stacy's Short Story Series

Sweet Romance about adult topics. Stories include: Finding Love on Christmas Vacation, Finding Love on the Summer Surf, Finding Love with Dear Santa, Finding Love with a Champagne Toast, Finding Love on the High Seas, Finding Love on a Dude Ranch, Finding Love at the Farmer's Market, Finding Love at the Coffee Shop

Heart of the Family Series

The *Heart of the Family* Series is a small-town steamy romance series that is best read in order. Books Include:

Mistletoe & Cocoa Kisses, Roses & Champagne Kisses, Orchids & Hurricane Kisses, Carnations & Hot Toddy Kisses,

Heal Me Series

Love Spicy Medical Romance? Check out the rest of the Heal Me Series for sexy romances that will warm your heart as they deal with life-altering medical and psychological issues. These books do contain language and open door sexual relations. While each book in the Heal Me Series is a stand-alone book, the characters cross between books and are best enjoyed by reading them in order. Books Include: Cured, Revived, Mended and Rescued.

The Celebration Series

The Celebration Series: Celebration Township is made for family, friends, falling in love, and don't forget celebrating the holidays. The first twelve books bring two people onto center stage as they overcome odds and figure out what their futures may hold. There is laughter, love, romance and even suspense when you join these couples as they each find a happily ever after over a holiday. The thirteenth book brings all twelve couples, and even a few special guests, into final focus as the first couple in Tangled in Tinsel prepares for their wedding one year after they met. Books Include: Tangled in Tinsel, Tears to Cheers, Heathens to Hearts, Rainbows Bring Riches, Sweet as Sugar, Making Mom Mad, Sparklers or Spankings, Raffles to Rattles, Flirting with Fireworks, Working Under Wheels, Masquerading at Midnight, Blessing & Beans, Velvet & Vows.

The Sometimes Series:

The Sometimes Series consists of three romances where the passion is a touch spicy and there is a hint of suspense is in the air. Sometimes You Win is a stand-alone story that ends with a Happy-for-Now ending. Sometimes you Lose, Book 2 of the series does end in a cliffhanger and Sometimes You Play the Game will finally give the couple a Happily Ever After. In all three books, you will find adult language and situations. Books Include: Sometimes You Win, Sometimes you Lose, Sometimes You Play The Game.

Pleasure Your Fantasies Series

The Pleasure Your Fantasies series is an ADULT Series with coarse language and intense sexual situations along with suspense. Books Include: Mistletoe Fantasies, Whispered Fantasies, Secret Fantasies, Conflicted Fantasies, Returning Fantasies, Arrested Fantasies, Discovered Fantasies, and Explosive Fantasies

List Updated 10/27/25

www.ingramcontent.com/pod-product-compliance
Lightning Source LLC
Chambersburg PA
CBHW022030240626

47154CB00007B/2350